A flash of blu
mirror made l

Officer Dylan Smith.

"Evening, Ms. McCloud. Did you rob a bank?" Dylan's voice was deeper than the youthful echo that still too frequently haunted her dreams.

"I just felt like taking a drive."

"At midnight?"

"Is that against the law?"

"No. But doing sixty-five in a forty-five-mile-an-hour zone is. But, you know I'm not going to ticket you."

"You'd ticket any other speeder. I expect the same treatment."

His laugh would have warmed some cold spot deep inside her heart if she hadn't steeled herself against it. "I don't think I've ever had a speeder actually demand a citation from me before."

"Then I'm free to go?"

He dropped his arm to his side, sighed and stepped back from the car. His voice was suddenly weary. "I've never tried to stop you from leaving."

Dear Reader,

Not only does Special Edition bring you the joys of life, love and family—but we also capitalize on our authors' many talents in storytelling. In our spotlight, Christine Rimmer's exciting new miniseries, VIKING BRIDES, is the epitome of innovative reading. The first book, *The Reluctant Princess,* details the transformation of an everyday woman to glorious royal—with a Viking lover to match! Christine tells us, "For several years, I've dreamed of creating a modern-day country where the ways of the legendary Norsemen would still hold sway. I imagined what fun it would be to match up the most macho of men, the Vikings, with contemporary American heroines. Oh, the culture clash—oh, the lovely potential for lots of romantic fireworks! This dream became VIKING BRIDES." Don't miss this fabulous series!

Our Readers' Ring selection is Judy Duarte's *Almost Perfect,* a darling tale of how good friends fall in love as they join forces to raise two orphaned kids. This one will get you talking! Next, Gina Wilkins delights us with *Faith, Hope and Family,* in which a tormented heroine returns to save her family and faces the man she's always loved. You'll love Elizabeth Harbison's *Midnight Cravings,* in which a sassy publicist and a small-town police chief fall hard for each other and give in to a sizzling attraction.

The Unexpected Wedding Guest, by Patricia McLinn, brings together an unlikely couple who share an unexpected kiss. Newcomer to Special Edition Kate Welsh is no stranger to fresh plot twists, in *Substitute Daddy,* in which a heroine carries her deceased twin's baby and has feelings for the last man on earth she should love—her snooty brother-in-law.

As you can see, we have a story for every reader's taste. Stay tuned next month for six more top picks from Special Edition!

Sincerely,

Karen Taylor Richman
Senior Editor

Please address questions and book requests to:
Silhouette Reader Service
U.S.: 3010 Walden Ave., P.O. Box 1325, Buffalo, NY 14269
Canadian: P.O. Box 609, Fort Erie, Ont. L2A 5X3

Faith, Hope and Family

GINA WILKINS

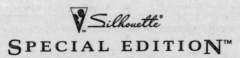

SPECIAL EDITION™

Published by Silhouette Books

America's Publisher of Contemporary Romance

For my mom, everybody's Nana.

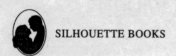 SILHOUETTE BOOKS

ISBN 0-373-24538-6

FAITH, HOPE AND FAMILY

Copyright © 2003 by Gina Wilkins

GINA WILKINS

is a bestselling and award-winning author who has written more than sixty-five books for Harlequin and Silhouette. She credits her successful career in romance to her long, happy marriage and her three "extraordinary" children.

A lifelong resident of central Arkansas, Ms. Wilkins sold her first book to Harlequin in 1987 and has been writing full-time ever since. She has appeared on the Waldenbooks, B. Dalton and *USA TODAY* bestseller lists. She is a three-time recipient of the Maggie Award for Excellence, sponsored by Georgia Romance Writers, and has won several awards from the reviewers of *Romantic Times*.

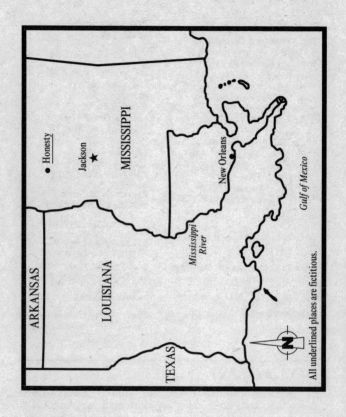

All underlined places are fictitious.

Chapter One

The Honesty city limits sign was just visible within the range of Deborah McCloud's headlights. She was tempted to keep driving, leaving the town where she had grown up behind her. Honesty, Mississippi, wasn't her home anymore; she had escaped nine years ago when she'd left for college, and she hadn't been back for more than a few days at a time during the past seven years. It was only because her mother and two older brothers still lived here that she returned at all.

Mostly her mother, she acknowledged. She and her brothers had drifted apart in the past few years.

It might have been a Freudian impulse that made her press harder on the accelerator as she moved closer to the edge of town. Probably a barely suppressed desire to escape the unhappy memories here, though she tried not to dwell on them during her infrequent visits with her mother. She supposed it was her brother's wedding that afternoon that had brought the memories so close to the surface tonight, preventing her from sleeping.

A flash of blue lights in her rearview mirror made her hiss a curse between her teeth. Terrific, she thought, pulling over at the side of the deserted road. The only thing that would make this episode worse was if the officer who had pulled her over was Dylan Smith. Surely, fate wouldn't be that cruel.

She should have known better.

Resting one hand on the top of her car, Dylan studied her through the open driver's-door window. Even though he was silhouetted by the yellowish street-lamps above him, she had no trouble picturing his roughly handsome face, nor his bitingly intense steel-gray eyes. The dark-brown hair he had once worn rebel-long was now almost militarily short, befitting his career on the right side of the law.

When he spoke, his voice was deeper than the youthful echo that still too frequently haunted her dreams, but it held the familiar undercurrent of mocking humor. "Evening, Ms. McCloud. Did you rob a bank? Knock over a liquor store? You seem to be in a big hurry to get out of town."

Knowing her face was illuminated by the same light that shadowed his, she kept her expression impassive. "I'm not leaving town. I just felt like taking a drive."

"At midnight?"

"Yes. Is that against the law?"

If her challenging tone annoyed him, he didn't let it show. "No. But doing sixty-five in a forty-five-mile-an-hour zone is."

"So write me a ticket." She extracted her driver's license from her wallet and held it out to him. "If you run this, you'll see that I have no outstanding warrants."

He made no move to take the license. "You know I'm not going to ticket you."

"You'd ticket any other speeder. I expect the same treatment."

Leaving his hands where they were, he asked, "How was your brother's wedding?"

The abrupt change of subject made her blink. She lowered her outstretched hand to her lap. "It was fine. No problems."

"Gideon and Adrienne make a great couple."

"Yes, they do." Keeping her voice totally disinterested, she said, "I heard that Adrienne insisted on inviting you. How come you didn't show up?"

"It's not like you to ask stupid questions."

His curt reply made her temper flare again. "Then I'm sorry I asked."

He sighed. "I didn't want any unpleasantness to cast a shadow over the wedding. I knew you wouldn't want me there. And, despite my new friendship with Adrienne, Gideon and I still barely speak. For their sake, and for your mother's, I didn't want to risk any problems."

"I really couldn't care less if you were there or not. And my mother would have been as gracious to you as she was to any of the other guests."

He obviously didn't buy her implication that he no longer had the power to stir any emotions, even negative ones, in her, but he didn't challenge her on that. "I always admired your mother, you know. A real class act. The way she's being so kind to her ex-husband's orphaned little girl—well, that just confirms what I always thought about her."

Deborah had no intention of discussing her family scandals with him. "I'm sure my mother would be pleased that you think so highly of her."

He made a sound that might have been a laugh. "I'm sure your mother couldn't care less what I think of her."

She tapped the steering wheel again. "Are you going to write me a ticket or not?"

This time his laugh was a bit more natural. The one that had always warmed some cold little spot deep inside her heart—and would have done so again if she hadn't steeled herself against it. "I don't think I've ever had a speeder actually demand a citation from me before."

She scowled. "Well?"

"No ticket. I'll just advise you to slow down for the remainder of your drive."

"Then I'm free to go?"

He dropped his arm to his side and stepped back from the car. His voice was suddenly weary when he replied, "I've never tried to stop you from leaving, Deborah."

Not trusting herself to speak, she put the car in gear and drove away, well aware that he remained where he was until she was out of his sight.

Deborah was up early the next morning, having managed only a few hours of sleep after returning from her midnight drive. Following the scents of coffee and freshly baked sticky buns, she wandered into the kitchen where her mother stood at the counter slicing fruit. Impeccable as always, Lenore McCloud was already dressed in a cream blouse and a tailored camel skirt. Her once-dark hair was now liberally streaked with gray. It was sleekly styled, not a strand out of place.

Conscious of her own tumbled, dark-blond hair, baggy T-shirt, plaid dorm pants and bare feet, Deborah cleared her throat. "I feel like I've walked into one of those old TV sitcoms. You're even wearing pearls."

Lenore reached up automatically to touch one of her earrings and then the gleaming strand at her throat. "I have a civic committee meeting this morning at ten. And the pearls match the outfit."

"Of course they do. You always match."

Lenore glanced at Deborah's outfit, but chose not to comment. "You were out rather late last night, weren't you?"

Deborah hadn't realized her mother had heard her leave. She should have known better. Pouring herself a cup of coffee, she replied casually, "I couldn't sleep. Decided to drive around for a while."

"Is there anything in particular on your mind? Something you would like to talk about?"

Carrying the coffee to the table in the cheery, bay-shaped breakfast nook, Deborah shook her head. "I guess I was still wired from the wedding."

Lenore joined her at the table, which was already set for breakfast for two. She set a plate of sticky buns and a bowl of fruit in the center, then fetched a cup of coffee for herself. "I'm so glad everything went perfectly yesterday. It was a lovely wedding, wasn't it?"

"Lovely." Deborah helped herself to a sticky bun, ignoring the fruit for the moment.

"Gideon looked happier than I've ever seen him."

"He did look surprisingly content, didn't he? Who would have believed he, of all people, would get involved in a whirlwind courtship and be married so quickly? What's it been, two whole months since he and Adrienne met face-to-face for the first time?"

Lenore smiled mistily. "It's nice to see both my boys so happy with their new brides."

Deborah plucked a pecan from the top of her bun, then popped it into her mouth. "Nathan's always happy."

"Well, not always, perhaps."

"C'mon, Mom, you know he's the sunniest-natured of your offspring. You long ago labeled me the temperamental one and Gideon the moody one. Nathan has always been the happy-go-lucky, optimistic older brother whose personal mission is to make sure the rest of us are safe and content."

"You and Gideon did tend to be more…challenging than Nathan," Lenore admitted. "But that doesn't mean I'm more partial to him—or to any of you. I love my children equally."

"I know," Deborah conceded. "And I'm glad you and Nathan were able to settle your differences. I know it was hurting you both when you were estranged."

Lenore smiled a bit wryly. "I could never stay angry with Nathan for long. No one could."

"Except me, of course," Deborah murmured into her coffee cup.

"Except you," Lenore agreed evenly, her smile deepening a bit.

"Still, you're sure you haven't gone overboard with this Isabelle thing? The way she tagged around behind you at the wedding yesterday, calling you 'Nanna,' treating you like her grandmother—that can't be a comfortable situation for you.''

Lenore pulled herself straighter in her chair, her green eyes snapping with what might have been annoyance. ''That's nonsense. I'm perfectly comfortable with the way things are. I know you've spent very little time around her, but Isabelle is an extraordinary four-year-old. She's bright, funny and well-behaved. And, since Nathan and Caitlin will be raising her with their own children, should they have any, she will probably always see me as a grandmother. Why would I mind that?''

Deborah could think of a half dozen reasons why—starting with the fact that Isabelle was the product of an extramarital affair between her father, former gubernatorial candidate Stuart McCloud, and a young campaign worker only a couple of years older than Deborah. The affair had become public only months before the election, putting an end to Stuart's campaign—and to his thirty-year marriage to Lenore, who had been both humiliated and devastated by the scandal. Still, Lenore had held her head high with characteristic dignity and poise.

A senior in an out-of-state college at the time, Deborah had never again spoken to her father after he left his family to marry his young mistress. Nathan-the-peacemaker had been the only one of the siblings to maintain a relationship with their father, though it had been a distant one since Stuart and Kimberly had moved to California to begin their new life together. Nathan was the only one who had visited Stuart there, where he had fallen hard for his little half sister.

When Stuart and Kimberly had died in a tourist accident in Mexico just over a year ago, Nathan had been named executor of the orphaned toddler's inheritance. And when arrangements for her care in California had fallen through, Nathan had brought her into his home, had himself appointed her guardian and announced his intention to raise her himself. With his new wife's help, of course.

Lenore hadn't accepted that development easily. At first, she had felt hurt and betrayed by Nathan's actions, refusing to have anything to do with the child. But when it had become apparent that Nathan's choice had been made and that she would push him away permanently if she refused to acknowledge the child who was now such an important part of his life, she had gracefully relented. Announcing that she would fill the role of surrogate grandmother for the child, she had once again earned the sympathy and support of her neighbors, who practically considered the generous, tireless community volunteer a saint.

There were times when Deborah wondered if her mother carried this sainthood thing too far. She was certain *she* couldn't have been so gracious in betrayal. In fact, she still harbored some resentment that Nathan had been willing to sacrifice his relationship with Lenore, Gideon and herself in favor of their father's late-life child. Even understanding his rationale—that Isabelle needed him more than the others did—didn't completely heal the wound. But then, she'd never claimed to be as noble as her mother, she reminded herself.

A real class act. Deborah could suddenly hear the echo of Dylan's voice when he'd spoken of Lenore only hours earlier. And she frowned, because she had been trying hard to put that awkward little interlude out of her mind.

Because she could tell that Lenore was becoming increasingly defensive about her decision to include Isabelle in her life, Deborah decided to change the subject. She would not allow her father's actions to cause another wedge between herself and her mother more than a year after his death. "I'm sure you know what's best for you," she murmured.

"What's best for me *and* for my family," Lenore concurred firmly. "And I won't let anyone else's opinion of my actions change my mind."

Deborah wondered if someone else had recently criticized Lenore's generosity toward her late ex-husband's child. Were there some who thought the local paragon had been a bit *too* saintly this time? If so, their opinions obviously made no difference to Lenore. Deborah decided to keep her own opinions to herself from now on, at least where Isabelle was concerned.

"I'm so glad you're staying a while this time." Lenore's smile was uncharacteristically misty for a moment, catching Deborah by surprise with the swift change of mood and subject. "It's been so long since you were home for more than a long weekend."

Thinking of her midnight run for the city limits, Deborah shifted guiltily in her seat. "It's nice to be home," she said, trying to infuse her voice with sincerity.

"Have you decided yet about your next job?"

Deborah shrugged. "I'm deliberating between offers in Atlanta and Dallas. I've enjoyed living in Tampa for the past couple of years, but it feels like time to move on."

Lenore shook her head. "You've lived in three different states since you obtained your degree less than five years ago. When are you going to settle down?"

"Hey, I'm single, unattached and in demand. Might as well try new experiences while I can, right?"

"I suppose so." Lenore looked doubtful. "But it does seem that you would want to start a family soon. You'll be twenty-seven in just ten days, you know."

"Yes, mother. I'm aware of my birth date and exactly how old I will be."

Her indulgent tone made Lenore smile a bit sheepishly. "Sorry. I suppose I have weddings and grandchildren on my mind these days."

"No wonder, with both Nathan and Gideon being married so recently. But you'll just have to be satisfied with those two weddings for a while. I'm in no hurry to complicate my life anytime soon."

"I hope my divorce from your father hasn't soured you on the prospect of marriage. Not every marriage ends so painfully. And even though mine did, I have no regrets. Your father and I had many happy years together, and I was blessed with three wonderful children. That more than makes up for any heartaches I might have suffered along the way."

Since her parents' divorce had been messy, humiliating and entirely too public, Deborah didn't know if she could ever reach the level of acceptance about it that Lenore had obtained. But then, she had never claimed to have her mother's seemingly endless supply of patience, generosity, tolerance and forgiveness. Lenore wasn't regarded as a saint in these parts without reason.

Because Deborah didn't want to talk about those

unhappy memories now, she abruptly changed the subject. "I'd like another cup of coffee. Do you want me to refill yours while I'm at it?"

"Just a half a cup, please—"

Before Deborah could even make it to the coffee-maker, the telephone rang. Both Deborah and Lenore looked at it in surprise. It seemed awfully early on this Saturday morning for anyone to be calling. Lenore moved to answer it.

Carrying both cups of coffee back to the table, Deborah opened the newspaper that had been sitting beside her plate and perused the headlines, making no effort to overhear her mother's end of the conversation. She had just turned to the comics page and was smiling at Garfield's shenanigans when Lenore rejoined her.

Deborah knew with one glance at her mother's face that the call had been bad news.

Her smile vanished as she set her coffee cup down with a thump. "What is it? What's wrong?"

For some reason, she had a terrible fear that something had happened to Gideon and Adrienne on their honeymoon. Irrational, of course, since Lenore looked sad, but entirely too calm for such a tragedy, but it was the first thought that popped into Deborah's mind. After all, her father had died while on a belated honeymoon with his second wife, though she was annoyed with herself for remembering that fact at that particular moment.

Lenore sank into her chair and reached for her coffee. "Caitlin's mother passed away during the night."

Deborah was immediately relieved that her brothers were unharmed. Still, she was genuinely sympathetic for her sister-in-law when she said, "I'm so sorry to hear that."

Lenore sighed, her eyes sad. "It's a blessing, I suppose. The poor dear hasn't even recognized her daughter for more than a year."

"Are Caitlin and Nathan going to Jackson to make the arrangements?"

"Yes, they're leaving later this morning. They'll be gone for two or three days while they organize the funeral and take care of other final arrangements. With this being a Saturday, there's not much they can do until business hours Monday morning. Staying in a hotel there will save them from having to be on the road a couple of hours a day, and Caitlin said she would rather be there with her mother until after the funeral on Monday. It will also put them in town to meet with the bank and the nursing-home administrator to settle all the bills and close out the trust funds Caitlin had set up for her mother's care. Isabelle will be staying here with us, by the way. Caitlin said that would be much more helpful to her than having us attend the funeral service."

Deborah set her coffee cup down with a thump. "They're bringing Isabelle here?"

"Of course. You wouldn't expect them to take a four-year-old to a funeral home, would you?"

What Deborah hadn't expected was to spend the next few days in the same house with her young half sister. It was awkward enough staying here, anyway, but at least when it was just her and her mother, she could concentrate on the happy memories of her childhood and deliberately refuse to think about the painful dissolution of her family.

That wouldn't be possible when she was sitting

across the breakfast table from the embodied evidence of her father's betrayal. As often as she had reminded herself that Isabelle was a permanent member of her family, and that the child couldn't be blamed for her parents' actions, it was still hard to be completely objective.

"No," she said a bit stiffly. "Of course they couldn't take Isabelle with them. But what about the housekeeper? Mrs. Tuckerman?"

"She isn't a live-in housekeeper. She's there during daytime hours. And besides, I volunteered to keep Isabelle. It will only be for a few days," Lenore reminded her. "They'll probably be back by Monday evening. And Isabelle really is no trouble at all. She's so behaved."

Deborah shrugged. "I'm sure it will be fine."

Especially, she added silently, since she intended to keep a polite, but definite, distance between herself and the child. Lenore would be the baby-sitter. Unlike the rest of the family—even Gideon, surprisingly enough—Deborah had no desire to form a close relationship with Isabelle. She simply wasn't comfortable with children, she told herself—particularly this one.

She had just finished her coffee when the doorbell rang. Lenore hurried to answer it, leaving Deborah to follow somewhat reluctantly. Caitlin, Deborah noted with a searching look at her sister-in-law's face, was sad, but composed, having resigned herself to this inevitability when her mother had suffered a massive stroke nearly two years ago. Nathan was a bit more subdued than usual, but his smile was still warm when he looked down at the blue-eyed and blond cherub clinging to his hand.

Deborah had been told several times that four-year-old Isabelle was the image of herself at the same age. She'd never known exactly how to respond to the observation, though she acknowledged the family resemblance. Dark-haired, green-eyed Gideon was the only one of Stuart McCloud's four offspring who hadn't inherited their father's bright blue eyes and golden hair. Despite common acceptance that dark hair and eyes tended to be dominant, Deborah had never been surprised that Stuart's genes had been as forceful and assertive as his personality. Nor did it seem odd to her that Gideon had been the one who was different even from conception.

She stepped toward Caitlin when Lenore moved away to speak to Isabelle. "I'm very sorry about your mother."

Caitlin squeezed Deborah's hand. "Thank you. I said goodbye to my mother a long time ago, of course, but I'll still miss my weekly visits with her at the nursing home, even if I doubt she ever knew I was there."

"Maybe she was aware you were there, but just couldn't let you know."

"Maybe some part of her did know me. It was that possibility that kept me going back every week."

Nathan slipped an arm around his wife's shoulders. "We'll be back in town in a few days," he told Deborah. "I hope we'll be able to spend a little time together before you take off again."

Family was extremely important to Nathan. Deborah knew that if it were up to him, he would keep everyone nearby where he could personally make sure they were all safe and happy. He would never fully understand Deborah's need to keep moving, content to live almost anywhere except the town where they had grown up.

Fifteen minutes later, Nathan and Caitlin were on their way. Thinking she would spend most of the day in the study with some correspondence and paperwork she needed to deal with, leaving Lenore and Isabelle to entertain each other, Deborah turned toward her mother. Lenore was checking her watch.

"I'll need to leave in ten minutes or I'll be late for my meeting," she said before Deborah could speak. "Isabelle, dear, I'll be out for a couple of hours, but you'll be fine here with Deborah."

Deborah cleared her throat somewhat loudly. "Um, Mother—"

"There's no need for you to worry about cooking lunch," Lenore rushed on, seemingly oblivious to the silent signals her daughter was trying to send her. "I'll pick up something on the way home."

"But, Mother—"

"I really must go," Lenore said firmly, her expression making it clear that she had received Deborah's signals but wasn't letting them deter her from her plans. "I'm the chair of this committee, and this is a very important meeting. Since you're here, anyway, there's really no reason you can't keep an eye on your sister for a couple of hours."

All too aware that Isabelle was watching the exchange with wide eyes and a somber expression, Deborah forced a faint smile. "Okay, sure," she conceded. "We'll be fine here during your meeting, won't we, Isabelle?"

The child nodded. "I'll be good, Nanna," she promised.

Lenore lightly patted the little girl's head. "I know

you will, dear. You always are.'' And then she pointed a finger at Deborah. ''You be good, too.''

Isabelle giggled.

Deborah gave another stiff smile. ''I'll certainly try.''

It seemed very quiet in Lenore's house after her whirlwind departure. Deborah glanced at the little girl gazing expectantly back at her and wondered what on earth she was supposed to do now.

How had this happened? She'd come here to attend her brother's wedding and then spend a few days with her mother. She had certainly never planned on *this!*

''So, um, what do you usually do on Saturdays?'' she asked.

Isabelle shrugged. ''Different things. We shop or go to movies or to the playground. Sometimes we go to the dog store.''

''The, um, dog store?''

Isabelle nodded, golden curls bobbing. ''To buy things for Fluffy-Spike, our dog. He's a bichon. Mrs. T. is going to feed him until Nate and Caitlin get back home.''

Deborah knew who Mrs. T. was—the indispensable Fayrene Tuckerman, who served as housekeeper, cook and daytime nanny in Nathan's busy household. But… ''Did you say Fluffy-Spike?''

Isabelle giggled again. ''I wanted to name him Fluffy and Nate kept calling him Spike because he thought it was a funny name for a little white dog, so now we call him Fluffy-Spike. That's funny, isn't it?''

It was the sort of name one would expect for a dog

belonging to Nathan, Deborah thought with a shake of her head. Her impulsive and often irrepressible eldest brother had rarely been accused of being predictable. He'd taken his little sister into his home as casually and impetuously as he had the recently adopted dog.

Isabelle had always called her older brother Nate. Lenore had told Deborah that there had been some discussion prior to Nathan's wedding of Isabelle calling Caitlin and Nathan Mom and Dad, since they would be raising her as their own, but that hadn't felt right to any of them. They had finally decided there was no reason Isabelle shouldn't call her brother and sister-in-law by their first names, though she was expected to obey them with the same respect she would have given her own parents.

It would be a casual, laughter-filled household, Deborah predicted. And yet there would be order, thanks to the briskly efficient housekeeper and to Caitlin, who was much more structured and organized than Nathan. Still, Deborah had been rather surprised by how well Nathan had adjusted to parenthood. He definitely indulged Isabelle, but stopped short of outright spoiling her. Deborah had heard him speak firmly to his little sister on a couple of rare occasions when she had needed correcting.

Deborah had no such confidence in her own childcare skills. She didn't have a clue what to do with the kid for the rest of the morning, for example.

Gossip traveled quickly through Honesty, and Dylan heard most of it courtesy of his aunt Myra, wife of his uncle, Owen Smith, the town's police chief. Myra could hardly wait to phone Dylan with the news that Nathan and Caitlin McCloud had been called out of town, leaving Lenore and Deborah to watch little Isabelle. Rumor had it that Deborah was baby-sitting that day while Lenore went about her usual busy Saturday schedule.

"I'm surprised Deborah agreed," Myra added. "She never forgave her father, you know, and most folks said she was pretty mad at her brother for bringing that little girl back here."

Dylan had no intention of discussing Deborah or her family with his aunt, who was well aware of the history between them. "Was there anything else you needed from me? Because I go back on duty in an hour and I—"

"No, that was all." Myra sounded disappointed that he hadn't risen to her gossip bait. "I just thought you would want to know what's going on with Deborah."

"It's really none of my business. I lost interest in the McClouds a long time ago, Aunt Myra."

It was a bald-faced lie, of course, he mused as he replaced the receiver in its cradle a few moments later. Though he'd made a massive effort to get over her, Deborah was the one McCloud who still interested him very much.

Not that he intended to do anything about it. Only a fool would deliberately stick his hand into the fire a second time.

Chapter Two

" . . . And my teacher's name is Ms. Montgomery, and I like her because she's nice. My best friends this week are Tiffany and Benjamin. Benjamin got lost in the woods at Cooper's Park for a long time, but Officer Smith found him. Danny made fun of Benjamin for getting lost and made him cry. I don't like Danny and Bryson because they're mean to me. They said my daddy was a bad man, but Nate and Gideon told me not to pay any attention to them."

Her fingers clenched around her coffee mug, Deborah gazed at the child on the other side of the kitchen table with somewhat stunned fascination. Isabelle had spent the last fifteen minutes eating an entire orange without pausing once in a seemingly endless monologue about her life in Honesty. Deborah had a hard time following everything Isabelle said—even though she had long since figured out that the only response required was an occasional nod or murmured ''mm-hmm''—but that last comment grabbed her attention.

''Who said what about your father?''

Licking a drop of orange juice from her lips, Isabelle answered easily, ''Danny and Bryson, mostly Danny. He doesn't say it much anymore because Miss Thelma said he had to miss playtime every time he talks about my daddy. Gideon told Miss Thelma to make Danny stop saying bad things about my daddy,'' she added.

''Um, Gideon did that?'' Deborah hadn't realized Gideon had ever gotten involved at Isabelle's school. After all, Nathan was officially Isabelle's guardian.

Isabelle nodded. ''It was when Nate and Caitlin were gone on their honeymoon and Nanna's sister got hurt so I had to stay with Gideon. I told him Danny said mean things about my daddy and he made me cry, and Gideon got really mad and he went to my school and talked to Miss Thelma and now Danny leaves me alone. Mostly.''

Deborah tried to picture the confrontation between her tactless, blunt-spoken brother and the equally forceful and intimidating owner of Miss Thelma's Preschool. It must have been quite a showdown, but she wasn't surprised that Gideon had accomplished his goal.

Realizing that Isabelle was studying her gravely from across the table, she asked, ''What is it?''

''Gideon said my daddy wasn't really a bad man, but some people got mad at him when he married my mommy and moved to California.''

Deborah frowned at her coffee cup, wondering what the child expected her to say. Obviously, Gideon had been trying to soothe Isabelle's feelings about her late father and he seemed to have done so with more sensitivity than Deborah would have expected from him. After all, Gideon had been estranged from their father for several years before Stuart's ultimate betrayal of the family. Like Deborah, he'd had no contact with Stuart during the three years before Stuart and his second wife died.

As for herself, Deborah had never talked to anyone about what her father had done to the family or her feelings about his death and she had no intention of starting now, with Isabelle. "You can always believe Gideon," she said instead. "He says exactly what he thinks."

"I know." Isabelle wiped her sticky hands on a paper napkin. "I saw some pictures of you with my daddy when you were little. Nanna showed them to me. She said I looked just like you when you were little. I liked the picture of you sitting on Daddy's shoulders. You were laughing and you had a red balloon. You know that one?"

The muscles in Deborah's face felt stiff when she nodded and replied somewhat curtly, "Yes, I know the one you mean."

She could picture the photograph as clearly as if it were sitting in front of her—herself at five or six, blond hair in pigtails, her expression pure joy as she rode her handsome, golden-haired father's wide, solid shoulders. He had been a god to her then, and she his little princess. Workaholic that he'd been, those leisurely family fun days had been rare and she had treasured every brief moment.

He had spent so little time with his first family, his days filled with business and the demands of his active political involvement. Yet he hadn't been too busy to start an affair with a young campaign volunteer even during his run for the governor's office, and Deborah had heard that he'd been a devoted husband and father to his second family. Rumor had it that the tragic vacation in Mexico had been the first time he and his second wife had spent any time away from their then three-year-old daughter.

Was it any wonder Deborah hadn't been enthused about having Isabelle become an integral part of her life? She didn't blame the child for their father's sins, but she couldn't help being reminded of them every time she saw a reflection of her own childhood innocence in the little girl's uncomfortably familiar face.

She glanced at the kitchen clock, wondering how much longer it would be before Lenore returned home. She couldn't take much more of this salt-in-old-wounds conversation with Isabelle. "Aren't there any TV cartoons you like on Saturday mornings?" she asked, seizing on the first distraction that popped into her head.

Isabelle shrugged. "We're usually too busy on Saturdays to watch TV."

"Oh. Well, since we're not particularly busy today, why don't you go see what's on? Mother should be home soon, and maybe she'll have something planned for you this afternoon."

"Okay." Isabelle stood obligingly. "You want to come watch TV with me?"

"No, thanks. I have some things to do. Just, uh, don't watch anything inappropriate."

When Isabelle gave her a puzzled look, Deborah

added, "Watch kid shows, okay? Cartoons or 'Sesame Street' or something like that."

As if she knew what kid shows were on TV these days, she thought as Isabelle left the room. None of her friends had children. Isabelle was the only child Deborah actually knew personally and theirs could hardly be described as a close relationship.

She stood to set her coffee cup in the dishwasher and throw away the peel from Isabelle's orange. She hoped her mother would be home soon.

Fate had not been very kind lately about granting Deborah's wishes. Lenore was detained by a crisis in her club that kept her busy for hours, leaving Deborah responsible for Isabelle for the entire afternoon.

Faced with trying to entertain the child herself for several hours or to let someone else do the entertaining, Deborah opted for the latter. "Why don't we eat a quick sandwich for lunch and then catch the Saturday matinee at the movie theater?" she suggested.

She wouldn't have to try to carry on a conversation with a four-year-old in a movie theater. Even if the film was completely inane, it seemed preferable to an entire afternoon of being studied by Isabelle's curious blue eyes. A couple of hours in a quiet, dark theater seemed very appealing to her just then; she could use the time to consider her options for her future.

It had been a very long time since she had attended a children's movie matinee.

A handful of popcorn hit her in the side of the head before the film even started. What seemed to be a full battalion of ear-splittingly noisy preadolescents dashed up and down the aisles, squealing and spilling sodas and snacks. Someone's cell phone played the

"William Tell Overture" in lieu of a ring, and a couple of babies wailed. Deborah shook her head in disbelief, wondering who'd bring either to a movie theater.

Seemingly accustomed to the chaos, Isabelle sat quietly in her seat beside Deborah, sipping orange soda and delicately munching her popcorn. Okay, Deborah thought, so the child was as well-behaved as Lenore boasted. That didn't mean Deborah wanted to spend any more afternoons baby-sitting.

The audience settled down—though only slightly—when the lights dimmed and the feature began. Just as Deborah resigned herself to watching animated animals singing and dancing for the next couple of hours, a few stragglers entered the theater, taking the empty seats in front of Deborah and Isabelle. The woman directly in front of Deborah was of average size, but the one who planted herself in front of Isabelle was very large and wore her hair in a high-teased bouffant that would have been stylish several decades earlier. Isabelle might as well have been staring at a blank wall.

"I can't see," she complained to Deborah, straining upward in her seat.

The rest of the theater was full; apparently, this was the premier of a highly anticipated family feature. "Switch seats with me," Deborah suggested in a stage whisper. "Maybe you can see better here."

The swap was accomplished easily enough, but it didn't make a difference. "I still can't see," Isabelle informed her, and this time her tone edged close to a whine. "Can I sit on your lap? Please? Nate lets me when I can't see."

The large woman with the big hair threw them a

stern look over her shoulder, accompanied by a hiss that let them know she wanted them to be quiet. Deborah bit her lip to hold in a remark that would have accomplished nothing but ill will.

"Stand up," she instructed Isabelle quietly. "We'll sit in that chair, since the view is less obstructed there."

She didn't bother to whisper the latter words. She was forced to find her small satisfactions where she could, she told herself as she returned to her former seat and helped Isabelle climb onto her knees.

"That's better," Isabelle whispered. "Thank you."

"Glad to oblige," Deborah muttered. And prepared herself for an uncomfortable couple of hours rather than the peaceful interlude she had envisioned at the start of this outing.

Dylan figured that everyone deserved a small vice or two. His was ice cream. His favorite flavor was butter pecan, but he occasionally indulged a craving for rocky road or strawberry. Most folks who knew him well were aware that he could often be found at the popular ice-cream parlor next to the mall Cineplex when he was on a break from duty.

The mall was predictably crowded on this nice Saturday afternoon in late May. Dylan was lucky to claim a small table in one corner of the ice-cream parlor just as a group of giggly teenagers abandoned it.

He had lived in this area for most of his life and had a highly visible job, so he knew quite a few of the other patrons. He greeted them with nods and waves before diving into his treat—a double scoop of butter pecan.

As he spooned a second bite of ice cream into his mouth, he thought of the only lawbreaker he had apprehended the night before. Deborah McCloud. He hadn't been prepared for that late-night encounter or for the flood of memories of other, more intimate midnight meetings between them.

Those memories had been haunting him ever since. It had been seven years, damn it. They'd been little more than kids when they broke up; he'd been barely twenty-three and Deborah had just turned twenty. You'd think he'd have put it behind him by now. God knew he had tried.

Yet all it took was one brief encounter with her to have him wanting her again.

He might have come a long way in the past seven years in a lot of respects, but when it came to Deborah McCloud, he was still an idiot.

A girlish shriek somewhere behind him drew his attention away from his ice cream. He turned just in time to catch the little blond rocket who launched herself into his arms.

"Hi, Officer Smith," she said, hugging him fiercely. "Where have you *been?*"

He chuckled as he returned the hug, then set the little girl on her feet in front of him. "Princess Isabelle. Aren't you looking pretty today in your royal purple?"

She patted her hair and preened a bit, showing off the purple knit T-shirt dress she wore with white socks and sneakers. "It's new," she confided.

"Very nice. But where's your tiara?"

She giggled. "I left it at home today."

"Ah. Traveling incognito this afternoon?"

"In…cog…?" She frowned in confusion. She was very bright for four, but that was a new word for her.

"Incognito," he repeated clearly. "Sort of means that you aren't calling attention to yourself."

"Oh." She smiled again. "I'm in-cob-neat-o."

"Close enough." He'd assumed she was there with Lenore McCloud, since he knew her guardians were out of town. Looking away from the child's beaming face, he was caught by surprise to find Deborah scowling at him over her little half sister's golden curls. "Oh. Hello."

Deborah looked a bit frazzled, he decided, trying to study her objectively. Her dark-blond shoulder-length hair was tousled, and there was a popcorn kernel stuck in a strand at the back. What might have been the beginnings of a tension headache had carved little V-shaped lines between her intriguingly winged dark brows.

It looked as though some dark liquid had splattered one leg of the jeans she wore with a thin, dark, scoop-necked sweater. When she moved to one side of Isabelle, he thought she dragged one foot a little, as though her leg had gone to sleep and was just tingling painfully back to life.

She was still the most beautiful woman he had ever known.

Isabelle gazed upward. "Deborah, do you know Officer Smith?"

"Yes. I wasn't aware that you knew him so well."

"He's one of my best grown-up friends," Isabelle replied happily. "Adrienne likes him, too, and so does Caitlin. And Gideon and Nate are being nice to him now because I told them to."

"I see."

It was obvious to Dylan that Deborah didn't at all see how he had suddenly become so friendly with her brothers, with whom he had a long history of animosity. Actually, *friendly* was a bit too warm a word to describe his new truce with her brothers, but he liked both her sisters-in-law. As a matter of fact, he and Gideon's literary-agent bride, Adrienne, had recently signed a business contract together, something he had no intention of mentioning just then.

As far as Dylan knew, Deborah hadn't been told that Dylan and her newest sister-in-law were now professional associates. Deborah didn't even know he had any aspirations other than being a small-town cop, working for his uncle, the police chief. He'd just as soon leave it that way for now.

"Deborah took me to the movie," Isabelle said, clinging to Dylan's knee. "A lady with big hair sat in front of me and I couldn't see, so I had to sit in Deborah's lap the whole time, and there was a baby who kept crying, and the boy beside us jumped up to cheer when the good guys won and he spilled his soda on Deborah's leg. It was fun."

Dylan knew better than to laugh, but it was a close call as he eyed Deborah's expression. He sincerely doubted that she would have described the experience as fun. "It was very nice of your sister to bring you to the theater," he said to Isabelle.

"Yes. And she's going to buy ice-cream cones because I told her Nate always buys ice cream when we come to the movies."

"Yes, well, we'd better let Officer Smith finish his own ice cream before it melts," Deborah said, avoiding Dylan's eyes.

Dylan hadn't realized quite how much Isabelle resembled Deborah until a very familiar, very stubborn look crossed the little girl's face. "I want to talk to him."

"We need to get home soon," Deborah countered. "Mother will want to see you when she gets home from her meeting."

"I'm staying with my nanna because Caitlin's mommy went to heaven, like my mommy and daddy did," Isabelle informed Dylan.

He spoke gently. "Yes, I heard."

"Will you come visit me at Nanna's house?"

Not a good idea, he thought with a glance at Deborah's forbidding expression. "I'm pretty busy with work right now, Princess Isabelle. But I'll visit you soon."

Her lower lip protruded a bit. "Deborah, tell Officer Smith he can come visit us. Maybe he could have dinner with us?"

What might have been consternation darkened Deborah's blue eyes. "Oh, I…"

Letting her off the hook, Dylan focused on Isabelle when he said, "I have to work tonight, Isabelle. But I promise I'll see you soon, okay?"

Isabelle didn't appear at all satisfied, but she finally nodded her head. "Okay."

Looking relieved now, Deborah reached down to take her little sister's hand. "Let's order our ice cream before the line gets too long."

"'Bye, Officer Smith."

"'Bye, princess. Nice to see you, as always, Deborah," he added dryly.

"Good afternoon, Officer," she returned, her voice chilly enough to refreeze his melting ice cream.

What kind of fool, he wondered as they moved away, carried a seven-year-old torch for a woman who could hardly stand to look at him?

A chance glimpse at the decorative wall mirror across the room gave him his answer.

He was that kind of fool.

Going to the movie had seemed like such a good idea at the time, Deborah mused as she combed her tangled hair, scowling at the popcorn kernel that fell to the floor. How could she have known what an ordeal it would become?

How could she have possibly predicted that they would run into Dylan?

Isabelle hadn't stopped chattering about him since they'd left the ice-cream parlor an hour ago. What a nice man he was. How kind he had been to Adrienne and Isabelle when they'd been involved in a minor traffic accident a couple of months ago. How strong he had been to carry Adrienne all the way to his patrol car when she hurt her ankle. How funny he was when he teased Isabelle and called her princess.

Apparently, Deborah wasn't the only McCloud woman to have succumbed to Dylan's lazy charms. It had been all she could do to prevent herself from warning Isabelle not to give her heart to the man; he would only turn around and break it. Shatter it into so many pieces that she would never be able to find all the parts.

The relationship between Deborah and Dylan had been too passionate, too complex and too volatile for her, as young and as sheltered as she'd been. At times, she had felt smothered, at others overwhelmed by the intensity of their feelings. Because of those factors, it had ended devastatingly—and perhaps inevitably, considering the differences between them. What few parts of Deborah's heart had been left intact after her breakup with Dylan had crumbled beneath the weight of her father's betrayal such a short time later.

"Deborah?" Lenore appeared in the open bedroom door, her smile both weary and apologetic. "I'm home. I'm sorry I've been gone so long."

Because Lenore looked so tired, Deborah didn't have the heart to complain about being left in charge of Isabelle. "That's okay. We managed."

"Yes, Isabelle told me you took her to a movie. That was nice of you."

Deborah shrugged and set the comb on the cherry dresser in her bedroom. "I didn't know how else to entertain her. She seemed to enjoy the outing."

"Yes, she was just telling me all about it. She had a lovely time. Um…she mentioned that you saw Dylan Smith at the ice-cream parlor."

Deborah scowled. "Yes. We saw him. Why on earth has Nathan let her get so attached to that…to Dylan?"

"I believe it all began while Nathan and Caitlin were on their honeymoon, when Isabelle was staying with Gideon and Adrienne. Dylan helped Adrienne when she was injured in a car accident, and the friendship grew from there. Adrienne seems to have grown almost as fond of Dylan as Isabelle—in a purely platonic way, of course," she added unnecessarily.

"I'm still surprised that Gideon doesn't object to his wife being buddies with one of his oldest enemies."

"Obviously, Adrienne is free to choose her own friends. And, actually, I think Gideon and Dylan are getting along a little better these days, which is a good thing, since they'll probably be interacting on occasion because of Adrienne. I wouldn't call Gideon and Dylan friends, exactly...."

"I would certainly hope not," Deborah muttered, appalled by the very idea.

"...but Gideon has become mature enough to put the past behind him. Gideon has probably realized how silly it is to carry a grudge for so long just because he and Dylan had a few confrontations in their schooldays. And Nathan was simply being the overprotective big brother when he objected to you being so intensely involved with Dylan at such a young and vulnerable age. But that all happened so long ago. I don't know why you can't let it go, as well—unless, of course, you still have feelings for—"

"I don't," Deborah snapped to prevent her mother from even finishing that sentence. "As I have told you plenty of times, the only feeling I have for Dylan Smith is extreme dislike."

"Well, I like him!" Deborah hadn't seen Isabelle appear in the doorway behind Lenore, but the angry outburst certainly got her attention. Isabelle was glaring at her, her little fists on her hips. "Officer Smith is my friend, and you should be nice to him like Nate and Gideon are."

"Isabelle." Lenore spoke quite firmly, a tone Deborah remembered very well from her own childhood. "We don't raise our voices like that. It isn't polite."

"And, besides," Deborah added when Isabelle subsided into a pout, "I was perfectly civil to your friend at the ice-cream parlor."

Almost nobly polite, in her own opinion. It hadn't been easy to resist the impulse to snipe at him, but she hadn't wanted to upset Isabelle. But she would be darned if she would answer to a four-year-old.

"Go wash your hands, Isabelle," Lenore instructed. "We'll be having dinner soon."

"That child is in danger of becoming spoiled," Deborah muttered when Isabelle shuffled away. "It seems that everyone in this family indulges her. Even Dylan."

Princess Isabelle, indeed.

"We *are* going to have to be careful," Lenore agreed. "She's had a rough time in her short life, being orphaned so young and moved around so many times. I suppose we try to overcompensate for that. I'm sure she's a bit unsettled today because Nathan and Caitlin have been called away, changing her routine again. Routines are important to four-year-olds, you know. And she really is very fond of Dylan."

"Fine. That's between her and Nathan, I suppose. But don't expect me to start cozying up to him just because the rest of the family doesn't want to hurt the kid's feelings."

Lenore took a step nearer to lay a hand against her daughter's cheek in a gesture that was as familiar as the no-nonsense tone she had used with Isabelle earlier. "You've never told me the details of your breakup with Dylan, but I know how badly it hurt you. And then your father broke your heart when he left us for Kimberly. He broke mine, too, you know."

Deborah swallowed a hard knot in her throat. "I don't—"

"You don't want to talk about it. I know. You never do. But I need to say one more thing. Better than anyone else in the family, I understand how hard it is for you to accept Isabelle into this household. Into our lives. I know what you see when you look at her. Don't you think I sometimes see it, too? I only agreed to accept her into our family when I realized that refusing to do so would place an insurmountable wall between Nathan and myself, something I simply couldn't allow. His kind heart wouldn't allow him to abandon his orphaned little sister when she had no one else to turn to, even if it cost him the rest of his family.''

"Okay, Nathan's a saint...."

"Hardly," Lenore murmured with a smile. "But he's my son, and I love him. So I accepted the child he will raise as his own. And, in doing so, I found my life immeasurably enriched. As hard as it may be for you—or for others—to understand, I've grown to love Isabelle very much. The joy and laughter and affection she brought with her replaced the anger and bitterness and hurt that I had lived with for so long. And it isn't just me. Nathan and Caitlin adore her, and even Gideon has learned to express his feelings more easily. It's impossible not to smile when Isabelle is around. We haven't forgotten how she was conceived, but we've put it behind us. And, in doing so, I think we've learned to forgive Stuart—to different degrees, of course.''

Blind instinct had Deborah moving back, away from her mother's tender touch. Away from the unexpressed request she simply couldn't fulfill. She would certainly never be cruel to Isabelle—to any child, for that matter—but she couldn't promise to accept the little girl the way the rest of the family had. Not if it meant forgiving what Deborah still considered to be unforgivable.

"I think I'd like to take a quick shower before dinner," she said. "I still have sticky cola all over my leg from the movie theater."

Lenore sighed, but didn't push, since she knew it would serve no purpose except to make Deborah more defensive. "All right. Dinner will be ready in half an hour."

Half an hour wasn't very long to repair a major crack in an emotional wall, Deborah mused as her mother left the room. But she could do it.

She'd done so plenty of times before.

Chapter Three

Lenore called Deborah to the telephone later that evening. Before Deborah could ask, Lenore added, "It's Lindsey Newman."

Deborah lifted her eyebrows in surprise. She couldn't imagine why a woman she hadn't seen in years would be calling her at her mother's house. "Did she say what she wants?"

"No, she just asked if you were available to speak to her. You can take it in the den, if you like. I'll be in the kitchen, making a cake for tomorrow's church potluck."

Deborah had been sitting in the den since dinner with her face buried in a thick book, leaving Lenore to help Isabelle with her bath, then read her stories and tuck her into bed. They'd all been perfectly courteous during dinner, Isabelle having returned to her sunny mood. Everyone had been very careful not to mention Dylan's name, but Deborah had been ready for time to herself by the end of the meal.

She picked up the phone to find out why her peaceful solitude had been interrupted. "Hello?"

"Deborah, hi. It's Lindsey Newman."

"Lindsey. It's been a long time." There was a question implied in the statement, a polite prompting for the reason for the call.

"I know. Except for seeing each other at the weddings, we've hardly had a chance to speak in the past few years. Seems like when you're in town, I'm always gone. Anyway, I know you're wondering why I called."

"Well, as a matter of fact…"

"I wanted to ask if you're free for lunch tomorrow. Or if not lunch, maybe dinner?"

Frowning in genuine bewilderment now, Deborah answered slowly. "Actually, I am free for lunch. My mother's got some sort of potluck thing at her church that I wasn't planning to attend."

"Great!" Lindsey's voice practically bubbled with satisfaction. "So can you meet me? How about pizza? It's been ages since I've had pizza."

"I suppose I can. Is there any particular reason we're meeting for lunch tomorrow or is it just for the pleasure of my company?"

Lindsey laughed. "Actually, there is a reason. But if you don't mind, I'd like to wait until tomorrow to discuss it with you."

"Okay, sure." Though still confused, Deborah was perfectly willing to meet Lindsey for lunch. They didn't know each other very well, Lindsey having been a couple of years ahead of Deborah in school, but Deborah had always liked the bubbly redhead.

She was sure their lunch would be much more entertaining than the church potluck her mother had been trying to talk her into attending.

She was still curious when she entered the designated pizzeria at one o'clock the next afternoon. They had chosen the time in hopes of avoiding the noon rush, but the place was still crowded. She was glad Lindsey had arrived early enough to have a table waiting when Deborah walked in.

Wearing a hot-pink jersey T-shirt with a hot-pink-and-orange flippy chiffon skirt, Lindsey stood to greet her. The colors should have been awful with her mop of red curls, but somehow it all worked, making Lindsey look bright and fresh and cheerful. In contrast, Deborah felt almost subdued in the red polo shirt she had paired with a short, straight khaki skirt.

"It's really good to see you," Lindsey said with a warm smile, her eyes sparkling with characteristic enthusiasm. "You look great, by the way. Love the hair."

"Thanks. You look good, too."

They took their seats at opposite sides of the booth, then chatted about inconsequential topics until they'd placed their orders and received their food. Lindsey was a close friend of Caitlin's and had been the maid of honor in her wedding, so she and Deborah had no trouble making conversation, though they had spent little time together in the past.

"I always thought Caitlin and Nathan would make a good couple," Lindsey said as she lifted a slice of Canadian-bacon-and-mushroom pizza. "Ever since he hired her as his partner in the law firm, there was always something special between them. Of course, when he took in your little sister, I wondered if Caitlin was prepared for a ready-made family, but it seems to be working out just fine.''

"Yes, the three of them seem very close.''

"I don't know if I would have the nerve to start out a new marriage with a three-year-old to raise. I've sort of made it a policy not to date guys with kids. Too many complications.''

"Exactly the way I feel about it,'' Deborah agreed, reaching for her soda.

Lindsey sighed. ''Not that I ever have time to date, as much as I travel for my job. Which, by the way, brings me to what I wanted to discuss with you.''

Deborah lifted an eyebrow. She knew that Lindsey was a sales rep for a local company; she believed they manufactured fishing lures or some such sports-related merchandise. She couldn't imagine what that had to do with her. ''Oh?''

"Yeah. Rumor has it you're between jobs right now.''

"In a way. I recently completed a contract in Tampa, and now I'm considering some other offers. But I really wouldn't be interested in selling fishing lures.''

Lindsey laughed and shook her head. ''I'm not suggesting you should. Actually, I'm considering opening a business here in Honesty, and I wondered if you would be interested in becoming a partner.''

Deborah set her plastic tumbler down to study the other woman in surprise. ''Really? What sort of business?''

"It would be a franchise store. A company based in Chicago is manufacturing a line of modular office furnishings—some of the coolest stuff I've seen on the market. I'm not sure if you're aware that my degree was in interior design. A long way from fishing lures, I know, but it's something I've always been interested in. I sort of stumbled into the sales job when I needed to pay off college loans. It's been so profitable, I've been slow to give it up, but now I'm ready to be self-employed and cut out some of the travel. Selling this furniture intrigues me, and since I know office design is your area…"

Deborah was technically considered an efficiency design consultant, her specialty being the maximization of office work space and effective traffic-pattern management. She didn't select colors or fabrics or furnishings as much as she arranged for the best use of limited space, and her services had been in increasing demand among growing businesses that weren't yet ready to expand into larger spaces.

She liked her job. Never too long in one place, no getting attached to people and then having to say goodbye. She much preferred dealing with blueprints and cutouts than trying to understand the complex workings of other peoples' minds.

"I know you've been freelancing, and I'm sure you like it that way," Lindsey rushed on when Deborah didn't immediately speak. "But, think about it. Wouldn't it be nice to expand the services you can offer? To provide modern furnishings that work well with your space-usage expertise? A partner to share the workload? To bounce ideas off?"

Deborah had certainly considered similar projects before. She had interned with several interior-design firms during college and had received offers during the past couple of years while she'd worked as a freelancer, primarily on word-of-mouth referrals.

She hadn't been getting rich, but she'd been living comfortably. Mostly, she'd been completely self-sufficient, dependent on no one, answerable only to herself, all of which had seemed very important to her since she'd left college.

"Surely you've noticed that this area is doing quite well business-wise?" Lindsey added, her pitch obviously well-rehearsed. "It's one of the fastest-growing areas in the state. Minority-owned businesses alone have increased by almost forty percent since nineteen—"

"Lindsey." Deborah decided it was time to interrupt before the other woman pulled out a PowerPoint presentation. "Why me?"

"Because you fit so well into the business plan I envision," Lindsey replied promptly. "I've followed reports of your career with both interest and envy. When Caitlin mentioned that you just finished a job and were considering new offers, it seemed the perfect time to approach you with mine."

"This has really caught me out of the blue."

"I realize that. And I hope you understand that I'm certainly not expecting an immediate answer. Take all the time you like to think about it; I've got to make a short sales trip early this week, anyway."

"To be honest, I hadn't planned to move back to this area. There's an advantage to quiet anonymity, you know."

Lindsey smiled in commiseration. "Don't I know it. Nearly everyone around here has known me all my life, and they feel that gives them the right to comment on my personal business whenever they like."

"Exactly. And it isn't as if my family hasn't had

its share of public problems,'' Deborah added in a mutter.

"I know. There will always be gossip, I suppose, but Nathan and Gideon seem to have risen above it very well. Nathan and Caitlin's law firm is thriving, and Gideon's really starting to hit it big with his writing. And your mother is certainly a highly respected member of the community.''

That understatement made Deborah grimace. "Yes, well, I'm not sure I want to take a place here among them. I rather like being completely on my own.''

"I've been on my own for a while, too—even though I still live in the town where I grew up. Sometimes it gets sort of…I don't know…lonely.'' Lindsey's somber expression lasted only a moment, and then she replaced it with her usual cheery smile. "But there are certainly advantages to it, as well. So take all the time you need to think about my offer. But promise me you will think about it.''

"I'll think about it,'' Deborah replied. Why not? Thinking certainly didn't involve obligation.

The brightness of Lindsey's smile increased by several watts. "Thanks. I've brought along a file full of catalogues and figures and projections—you'll find I've been doing my homework.''

"Apparently so.''

A tall, broad-shouldered man with fussily styled, thinning light-brown hair, sun-narrowed blue eyes and a shark's smile paused beside their table. "Well, hey, Deborah. Looking good. Haven't seen you around in a while.''

Deborah gave him a sidelong glance. "Let's keep it that way a while longer, shall we?''

Lindsey giggled.

Kirk Sawyer, former pro football player turned pitchman for his father's automobile dealership, scowled. "You always were a snotty bitch."

"And I've gotten even better at it since you used to annoy the hell out of me in school. Don't hang around and make me demonstrate it."

He snorted and turned to stalk away. His arrogant footsteps weren't quite steady; Kirk was rapidly becoming the town drunk, even though he still thought of himself as the local hero.

It hadn't been ruined knees alone that had destroyed Kirk's athletic career, though he would never admit that his problems had run much deeper. His daddy took good care of him, Deborah thought with a shake of her head. It was because of Bill Sawyer's pleas that Nathan had reluctantly defended Kirk in several DUI cases, until he'd finally had enough and refused to serve as Kirk's lawyer.

"Way to go, Deborah," Lindsey murmured. "That guy gives me the creeps. He made a heavy pass at me at a club one night. Thought I was going to have to pull out the pepper spray, but Dylan Smith was there to help me out."

"Of course he was." Former bad boy Dylan had somehow become the new local hero, Deborah thought, bemused by the reversals of fortune.

"Enough business. Let's rehash your brother's wedding."

Smiling at the abrupt change of subject, Deborah asked, "Which brother? They've both had weddings this year."

"The latest. Gideon. Everyone was so surprised when he suddenly up and married his New York agent. Word is they're going to split their time between Honesty and New York—mostly Honesty, since everyone knows how much Gideon hates having lots of people around.''

''Yes, that's their plan.''

''Adrienne seems confident she can handle her clients' business from here, for the most part. She told Caitlin she's going to cut back to just a select few. Gideon, of course, and a couple of other long-time clients. And now Dylan. That was certainly a shock.''

A half-eaten slice of pizza fell from Deborah's suddenly nerveless fingers, landing with a splat on her plate. ''What on earth are you talking about?''

''Dylan Smith. You haven't heard yet? Dylan hasn't said much about it, but you know how word gets around. Yolanda Krump found out that Adrienne has agreed to represent Dylan for a novel he has written. Yolanda's sister works at the post office, you know. She's the one who let the news slip. Yolanda is irate, of course, because Adrienne declined to represent that rambling so-called work of autobiographical fiction Yolanda's been babbling about for ages.''

''Dylan's written a book.'' It was the only part of Lindsey's explanation Deborah could focus on just then. ''And Adrienne's representing him.''

''Kicker, isn't it? Especially since everyone knows he and Gideon have never exactly gotten along. And now Gideon's wife is his agent *and* Dylan's. One of those small-world things.'' Lindsey took a sip of her cola, then suddenly tilted her head. ''You and Dylan were once an item, weren't you?''

''A long time ago,'' Deborah muttered, well aware that Lindsey already knew. ''Back when we were just kids.''

"So did you know then that he had aspirations of being a writer?"

"No."

"Ironic, isn't it, that he and Gideon have so much in common, really? Both good-looking guys, close to the same age, both writers."

"Lindsey."

"Mm?"

"If you want me even to consider a business partnership with you, you have to promise one thing."

"Which is?"

"We don't talk about Dylan Smith."

"Oh." Lindsey's expression turned speculative. "Sore subject?"

"You could say that."

"So, um, Dylan who?"

Deborah nodded in satisfaction. "Exactly."

Deborah was fuming when she stormed into her mother's house. During the drive back, she had tried very hard to concentrate on Lindsey's business offer, but her thoughts kept circling back to the same infuriating point.

"Mother!"

Lenore appeared in the living-room doorway with an expression that conveyed both curiosity and displeasure. "Honestly, Deborah, there's no need to shout. How was your lunch with Lindsey?"

"Did you know Dylan Smith has written a book? And that Adrienne is going to represent him?"

Lenore frowned. "I suppose Lindsey told you that. I wonder where she heard it."

"You didn't answer me. Did you know?"

After only a momentary pause, Lenore nodded. "I

knew. I thought it was still a secret in town. I should have known better. I wonder how Lindsey found out.''

''What I would rather know is how—and when—*you* found out.''

''I bet it came from the post office. Dylan had to mail several things to Adrienne's New York office, and you know what a bunch of gossips those folks are who've been working in our post office for the past thirty years. Especially Yolanda Krump's sister Twyla. She probably told Yolanda, who spread it all over town.''

Deborah's hands drew into fists at her hips. ''Would you please answer my question? How long have you known about Dylan's writing?''

''Not very long. Gideon told me. Adrienne seems confident that she's going to be able to sell Dylan's work, so it will become common knowledge eventually. Gideon figured he might as well tell me about it before the gossip broke—though it seems he barely beat it.''

''How could Adrienne do this to us? And why did Gideon let her? Surely he told her our family hasn't exactly been friendly with Dylan.''

''Honestly, Deborah, I can't believe what I'm hearing from you.'' Lenore shook her head in disapproval. ''To think that you, of all people, would suggest that a husband has a right to interfere in his wife's business decisions or to forbid her from making a decision. Just as Adrienne has a right to have Dylan for a friend, she certainly has every right to represent him if she considers him a potentially valuable client.''

With a wince, Deborah cleared her throat. "That wasn't what I was saying…exactly."

"Then what, exactly, did you mean when you asked why Gideon *allowed* Adrienne to accept Dylan as a client?"

Deborah gave a gusty sigh and shoved a hand through her hair. Because there was no way to clarify her outburst without making it worse, she asked, instead, "Why didn't you tell me?"

"I'd been asked to keep it confidential for the time being. I don't spread secrets or gossip."

"You could have told me," Deborah said quietly. "Especially me. You shouldn't have let me find out like this."

Her mother's expression changed from annoyed to regretful. "I'm sorry, Deborah. I didn't realize it would matter quite this much to you."

Deborah drew her shoulders straight and lifted her chin. "It doesn't matter that much," she lied. "I just don't like hearing family business from outsiders."

"I can understand that. But you really shouldn't let it worry you, dear. Adrienne certainly won't be bringing her clients home for dinner. You won't have to deal with Dylan any more than you have for the past few years. After all, he didn't even attend Gideon and Adrienne's wedding."

Regretting now that she had allowed her emotional control to slip, Deborah masked her feelings behind an impassive expression and a shrug. "Where's Isabelle?" she asked, firmly changing the subject.

"She's in the kitchen making a collage with magazine cutouts and scraps of fabric, rickrack and buttons. It's a terrible mess, of course, but she seems to be enjoying herself."

"I'm sure she is. I think I'll go catch up on my e-mail."

"I'll call you when dinner is ready."

"Thanks." Suddenly eager to be alone—even if it meant she was a terrible houseguest—Deborah turned and left the room.

She should have spent the afternoon thinking about Lindsey's unanticipated business proposition—and she did, a bit. She thought especially about how accepting the offer would mean spending more time in Honesty, most likely increasing the amount of time she would spend around Isabelle and the number of occasions on which she would encounter Dylan.

A writer. She growled beneath her breath and plopped down heavily on the side of her bed. She had just gotten accustomed to thinking of the former teenage bad boy as a respectable officer of the law. And now this?

As irrational as she knew she was being, she couldn't help suspecting that he had done this just to get under her skin. And probably Gideon's, as well. After all, Gideon had been published for several years, his thrillers having built a loyal and enthusiastic following. It had been through his writing that Gideon had met Adrienne, his agent of two years. When she'd visited him here in Honesty for business purposes a few months ago, their first face-to-face meeting, they'd fallen in love almost immediately.

Now Gideon and Adrienne were away on their honeymoon and Deborah had discovered that Dylan was also one of Adrienne's clients. What was she to make of that?

Nothing, she told herself. It was none of her business. If Gideon was okay with having Dylan Smith as part of his wife's life, Deborah had no reason to get involved. Except for the inevitable small-town encounter, Dylan was completely out of her life now.

Exactly the way they both wanted things to remain.

Isabelle attended preschool the next day, and Lenore had her usual busy calendar, so Deborah was alone in the house for several hours, something she assured her mother she didn't mind at all. She spent the morning studying the thick file of materials Lindsey had provided about the furniture franchise. She had finally succeeded in putting Dylan out of her mind, for the most part, and she was able to concentrate on business, except for three annoying incidents when the phone rang, but no one was on the other end of the line. Telemarketers, she assumed, hanging up irritably after the third non-call. She shared Gideon's extreme dislike for the pesky profession.

She had to admit that Lindsey's proposition was intriguing. She spent a long time leafing through catalogs of furnishings, and she liked what she saw. The furniture was of as high a quality as Lindsey had claimed, combining versatility with clean, modern styling. She could envision these pieces fitting very well into her clients' decor and daily usage.

Sales wasn't Deborah's area, but Lindsey was apparently good at it. With Lindsey's sales expertise and Deborah's design experience, she could see how they could build a successful business.

She just hadn't convinced herself she was interested in making that sort of long-term commitment. Nor in working with a partner. As much as she liked Lindsey, how was she to know Lindsey could be depended on for the long run?

Deborah had learned from experience that it wasn't always wise to put her faith in others, no matter how likeable or trustworthy they might initially appear to be.

Finally, driven from her room by hunger, she wandered toward the kitchen for a late lunch. She was a bit surprised to find her mother standing beside the kitchen counter, her back to the doorway Deborah had stepped through.

"Hi, Mother. I didn't realize you were back."

Lenore gasped, jumped and whirled around.

"Sorry," Deborah said, holding up both hands in apology. "I didn't mean to—what's wrong?"

Lenore's face was unnaturally pale, and her mouth was drawn into a tight line. She clutched a single sheet of paper in her unsteady right hand. "You startled me. I didn't hear you come in."

Deborah wasn't buying it. "What are you holding?"

"I, um—" Lenore looked down and Deborah would have sworn her mother's face lost even more color. "It's nothing."

She didn't accept that, either. Because every fiercely protective filial instinct she possessed had just kicked into overdrive, she held out her hand, speaking in the no-nonsense voice she had learned from Lenore. "Let me see."

"It's just some small-minded busybody's attempt to throw her—or his—weight around. Someone who gets a sick sense of power by intimidating other people."

"Let me see," Deborah repeated patiently.

Sighing, Lenore held out the paper. "It's trash, of course. Nothing at all to worry about. I shouldn't have even given it a second thought, much less let it upset me.''

Deborah scanned the terse paragraphs with a hard knot of anger forming in her chest. ''When did you get this?''

''It was in today's mail. No return address, just an Honesty postmark, dated Saturday.''

''And this is the first time you've gotten anything like this?''

When Lenore didn't immediately respond, Deborah looked up with narrowed eyes. ''Mother?''

''It's not the first,'' Lenore admitted reluctantly. ''But it's the most unpleasant.''

''How many?''

''Three—maybe four. I don't know. I threw them away.''

''Has there been anything else? Phone calls? Any other personal contact?''

''No. Just the letters. I'm sure there's nothing to worry about.''

''You're probably right.'' But she agreed only to ease the lines around her mother's mouth. Deborah was furious and, no matter what she'd just said, she was worried.

As much as she hated it, there was only one person she could think of to turn to for advice.

Dylan's mobile home was old but in good repair, and he kept it relatively neat, for a bachelor. It sat on three partially wooded acres that backed up to a small fishing lake just outside of town, giving him a nice view of the water from the wooden deck he'd built across the back of the trailer. He'd bought the place two years ago with vague plans of building a house here someday. When he was ready.

He had the money to build now, if he wanted. But, as he told all those who asked what he was waiting for, he wasn't ready. There never seemed to be any urgency to build a house just for himself, and he hadn't met anyone in the past few years he wanted to ask to share it with him. His dogs were company enough for now.

It was the barking of the dogs that let him know he had company Monday afternoon. Glancing at the clock, he saw that it was just after two, an unusual time for anyone to come calling. Putting away the lunch dishes he'd just finished washing, he wiped his hands on a dishtowel, tossed it on a counter and headed for the front door just as someone knocked.

If there was one person he would not have expected to find on his top step, it was Deborah McCloud.

Seeing her at his door, her blue eyes meeting his with the direct challenge with which she had always faced him, her dark-blond hair tossing in the spring breeze, it suddenly occurred to him exactly what he'd been waiting for all this time.

Chapter Four

In Dylan's job, it was necessary for him to hide his emotions when he was caught off-guard. It took him a bit longer than usual to conceal his reaction to finding Deborah McCloud at his door.

His brief delay in greeting her caused her to speak impatiently. "Has the sight of my face turned you to stone or are you just trying to tick me off?"

Confident now that she could read nothing but lazy amusement in his expression, he leaned against the door frame. "I was trying to imagine what could have brought you to my home. I've got to admit, no credible explanation is coming to me."

"Just let me make it clear that this visit has nothing to do with anything that happened in the past. Between you and me, I mean. I'm here strictly because I need to ask your advice in your capacity as a police officer."

That drained the humor out of him. "Come in."

Though she held her head high when she walked past him, the stiffness in her shoulders told him she would rather be just about anywhere else but here. The fact that she *was* here was what had him concerned. Something must be seriously wrong for her to come to him for help.

She crossed straight to the glass doors at the back of his living room, looking past the small wooden deck to the glittering lake beyond. "Nice view."

"Thanks. That's why I bought the place."

She turned then to glance around the room, and he saw his home through her eyes. Clean, yes, but a bit shabby—few decorations, fewer luxuries. He just hadn't bothered. It was certainly not what the daughter of a prominent businessman and a dedicated socialite was accustomed to. The difference in their social status had always been an issue between them, more on his part than hers, he had to admit.

But she wasn't here about the past, he reminded himself.

"You want a soda or something? Coffee, maybe?"

"No." And then she made herself add, "Thank you."

"At least have a seat."

After hesitating only a moment, she perched on the edge of a nubby green armchair—a hand-me-down from his aunt Myra. Dylan settled on the green plaid sofa. "Tell me what happened."

"Someone has been threatening my mother."

That brought him sharply upright. "What the hell?"

Digging in the soft leather bag she'd brought in with her, she pulled out a sheet of paper. "This came in today's mail. She said she's received a few others prior to this one, but she threw them away."

He scanned the unsigned letter rapidly. "Were the other letters identical to this one?"

"She said this one was more unpleasant, to use her word."

"So you believe the sender's outrage is escalating."

"That's what I came to ask you. Am I overreacting, or should I be concerned?"

"Anonymous letters are always cause for concern, though there's certainly no reason for panic at this point." He looked up from the letter to Deborah's grim face. "Have you discussed this with your brothers?"

"No. As I said, the letter just arrived today. Gideon's on his honeymoon and Nathan won't be back in town until later today."

"So you came straight to me?"

She leveled a frown at him. "I told you. I came to you as a cop. I called the station, and they said you were off duty, so I thought this would be a good time to discuss it with you. Off the official record, of course."

She had to have swallowed a great deal of pride to make this visit, he figured. It was a measure of her love for her mother that she had done so. Because of his own admiration for Lenore McCloud, he was scowling when he returned his attention to the letter.

"I would like to talk to your mother and ask her about the other letters, who she knows who might have sent them."

"I asked her that, of course. She said she couldn't think of anyone. She didn't want to discuss it at all, actually. When she left to pick up Isabelle from pre-school, I decided to consult with you.''

He nodded. ''For what it's worth, I think you did the right thing. This is probably nothing to worry about, but it's something I'd like to keep a handle on. I'll hang on to this letter for a few days. You think your mother would talk to me?''

''You could try. She asked me not to mention anything to Nathan or Gideon—she doesn't want to disturb them—but she didn't say anything about talking to you.''

His smile felt lopsided. ''Probably because she never considered the possibility that you would.''

''Only for my mother's sake,'' she muttered without looking at him.

''I never suspected any other reason,'' he answered wryly.

She pushed herself abruptly to her feet. ''So you'll look into this?''

He rose more slowly. ''You knew I would when you came to me.''

Shoving her hands in her pockets, she nodded and moved toward the door. ''Thanks.''

Her hand was on the doorknob when he spoke without actually planning to do so. ''You're never going to forgive me for the things I said that night, are you?''

He watched as she stiffened. Her answer was barely audible. ''No.''

''Even though they later proved to be true?'' he asked, knowing he was risking a flare-up of Deborah's notorious temper.

What he got, instead, was a quiet, ''Especially because of that.''

She'd closed his front door behind her before he could have answered. He was still shaken by the realization that there had been a hint of tears in her voice.

She was more upset than she wanted to admit about the letter her mother had received. And he was ruefully aware that he would do anything she asked him to do, even though she still hated him.

Knocking on Dylan's door had been one of the hardest things Deborah had ever done. For nearly five minutes she'd sat in her car outside his trailer, watching two rather goofy-looking mutts running back and forth in a fenced side yard, barking their silly heads off while she had debated driving away. Only the memory of her mother's stricken expression could have made her open her car door and walk up Dylan's path.

He probably thought he'd hidden his surprise at seeing her there. His hard-carved face had gone carefully blank, his left eyebrow had risen and his voice, when he'd finally spoken, had been a sardonic drawl. But she had seen the startled look flash through his steel-gray eyes when he saw her, and she knew he wasn't as blasé as he'd appeared.

Had he, too, been forcibly reminded of the afternoons when they had slipped away to be alone together? Had those memories been as painful for him as they were for her?

You're never going to forgive me for the things I said that night, are you?

Wrapping her arms around herself as if to ward off a sudden chill, she entered her mother's kitchen more than an hour after she'd left Dylan's mobile home.

She had spent some time just driving around town, finding the familiar places of her childhood, wondering how anyone here could be so hateful as to write the things she had read in that letter.

Lenore was cooking—something she often did when she was perturbed. The pleasant smells of apples and cinnamon filled the kitchen, bringing back even more memories for Deborah. It seemed to be a day for them.

"Are you okay?" she asked.

Lenore glanced around. A tiny smudge of flour streaked her left cheek, making her look uncharacteristically disheveled. "Yes, I'm fine. I'm making an apple cobbler. I haven't made one in quite a while, have I?"

Deborah looked around the empty kitchen. "Where's Isabelle?"

"She's playing in the backyard. She took a big spoon and a saucepan and said something about digging for worms in the flower bed."

The fenced backyard was big and shady, a perfect place for a child to play, as Deborah could have attested from her own childhood. "Good. I wanted to talk to you without her hearing."

"Where have you been?" Lenore asked as she slid the cobbler pan into the oven.

"I went to Dylan Smith's house."

Lenore straightened slowly, then turned to face Deborah, her expression a mixture of shock and disapproval. "Don't you think that was an overreaction?"

Deborah leaned against a countertop. "No."

"Why on earth would you go to Dylan when

you've just told me that you never wanted to see him again?"

"I didn't go to see Dylan. I went to talk to a police officer about something disturbing that happened to you. Since Honesty doesn't have an abundance of police officers to talk to, I chose the only one I actually know."

Crossing her arms, Lenore studied her. "What did he say?"

"That he would like to speak to you, if you'll agree. He wants to ask you a few questions."

"I have no answers for him. I can't imagine who has been sending those letters, who dislikes me enough to want to upset me this way."

Deborah shook her head. "Not you, Mother. Whoever sent these letters hates Dad and, because of him, Isabelle. They thought you would refuse to accept her and that she would have to find another place to live. But Nathan is a prominent attorney in town, and you're a highly respected community leader. When you gave your approval to his taking her in, even acknowledged her as a member of your family, you secured her a place here in Honesty. Whoever sent the letters can't stand the thought of that."

Lenore's face had gone grim in response to Deborah's blunt and deliberate recap of the letter's angry message. "I know what was said."

"Do you also remember the threat at the end of the letter? Something about how sorry you'll be if you keep 'shoving the kid down everyone's throat'?"

"I remember every word. I just don't believe there's any real danger."

"And I hope you're right. But we would be foolish

to ignore the letter without taking some precautions. Will you talk to Dylan?''

''I'll answer the few questions that I can. That won't be much.''

''It's all I ask.''

Lenore had already turned to rummage in the refrigerator. ''I think I'll bake some pork chops for dinner. Does that sound good to you?''

Knowing there would be no more talk about the letter for now, Deborah shrugged. ''Anything is fine with me. Is there anything I can do to help?''

''Would you check on Isabelle for me? She went out only a few minutes before you got home.''

''Sure.'' Deborah headed obligingly for the back door.

It occurred to her then that she had been so focused on the potential threat to her mother that she hadn't given much thought to the letter writer's hostility toward Isabelle. But it was in her mind as she went to check on the child. While Deborah still had mixed emotions about Isabelle, she couldn't imagine why anyone outside the family would be so adamantly opposed to the child's presence here.

Okay, Deborah had initially advised Nathan to find Isabelle a good home in California. She had thought it would be easier for everyone, especially for her mother. She had even convinced herself it would be better for Isabelle, whom she hadn't even met at the time. After all, Nathan had still been single then, and Deborah had thought Isabelle would be better off with a two-parent family. In Honesty, she had insisted, Isabelle would always live under the shadow of gossip about her parentage.

Deborah wouldn't deny that there had been a selfish angle to her resistance. She'd been content with her family as it had been—her mother, her brothers and herself. She hadn't wanted to face her father's youngest child on a regular basis. She hadn't wanted to be forced to examine her own sternly repressed feelings about the past, as she feared she might eventually have to do now that Isabelle was an integral part of the family circle.

She walked outside, telling herself that she had come a long way since her initial opposition to Nathan's guardianship of Isabelle. While she hadn't exactly bonded with the kid, they were friendly enough to keep things pleasant. And now that Isabelle was a part of the family, Deborah took great exception to anyone making threats against her.

"Isabelle?" She glanced around the neatly manicured lawn. Spring flowers were in bloom in Lenore's well-tended beds, and Deborah scanned them for signs of a little blond worm-digger.

"Isabelle?" A flagstone walkway wound around a concrete birdbath and behind a small white-sided storage building. Deborah followed it around, enjoying the scented breeze on her face. "Isabelle, whatcha' doing? Have you found any good worms?"

There was no answer.

Sighing impatiently, Deborah placed her hands on her hips and looked around. "Okay, Isabelle, your hide-and-seek game is very amusing, but it's time to come out now. Nanna's making apple cobbler. Doesn't that sound good?"

When nothing but silence greeted that question, she felt the muscles in the back of her neck begin to knot. "Isabelle?"

Catching a glimpse of something shiny in one of

the azalea beds, she hurried toward it. Kneeling in front of the bed, she picked up a dirt-encrusted stainless-steel spoon and a small saucepan with a half-inch of mulch in the bottom. Isabelle was nowhere to be seen.

Cautioning herself to remain calm, Deborah went back into the house after making certain Isabelle wasn't hiding anywhere in the backyard. She stopped first in the kitchen. ''She's not outside. She must have come in.''

Frowning a little, Lenore wiped her hands on a dishtowel. ''That's odd. I didn't see her.''

''I guess she slipped past us.'' Moving to the hallway that led out of the kitchen, Deborah raised her voice. ''Isabelle?''

''She must not have heard you.'' Lenore moved past Deborah, heading for the foyer. ''I'll check upstairs. You look down here. Perhaps she's watching television in the den.''

Five minutes later, they met again at the foot of the stairs, their search fruitless. Lenore's right hand was shaking when she lifted it to her throat. ''Are you *sure* she wasn't in the backyard?''

''I'm positive. I looked everywhere.''

''Was the gate open?''

''No, it was closed. I checked.''

''Oh, my God.''

Haunted by the memory of that anonymous letter, Deborah turned grimly toward the den. ''I'm calling the police.''

Lenore McCloud was not a woman who panicked easily. Deborah had seen her mother remain calm through numerous crises and emergencies. Even during the scandal of Stuart's aborted campaign, Lenore hadn't shown anyone the full extent of her pain, withdrawing into her room until she was certain she could emerge with her head high and her emotions masked.

Lenore hadn't meant to push her children away when they'd needed her most, Deborah thought. It had simply been Lenore's way of dealing with her humiliation.

Yet Lenore was unable to conceal her panic in response to Isabelle's disappearance. Wringing her hands, she paced her kitchen. "What are we going to do?"

Standing on the other side of the room, Deborah looked at her watch. As far as they knew, Isabelle had been missing for approximately forty minutes. Deborah had called the police less than ten minutes ago, but her mother's house wasn't far from the police station. They should be arriving any minute.

As if on cue, the front doorbell rang. She and Lenore both hurried to answer it.

The moment Lenore opened the door, Dylan stepped into the foyer without waiting for an invitation. His rugged face was deeply creased, narrowing his eyes to hard gray slits. He had on his uniform now, rather than the jeans and T-shirt he'd worn when Deborah had left him at his place. His navy-blue shirt was crisp, adorned with identifying patches, his name tag and his badge. Around the waist of his sharply creased navy slacks was a utility belt from which dangled his weapon, stick, radio and other tools of his trade that Deborah couldn't immediately identify. Dressed like this, his expression grimly professional, he looked rather more intimidating than Deborah was accustomed to seeing him.

When he spoke, his words were directed toward Deborah. "What happened?"

She had an irrational urge to hold on to his arm, as if to find reassurance in his strength. Clasping her hands tightly in front of her, instead, she spoke huskily, "Isabelle was playing in the backyard. When I went out to check on her, she was gone. We've looked everywhere."

Sharing none of Deborah's compunctions, Lenore clutched Dylan's forearm in both her hands. "That letter," she said. "Do you think—?"

He covered her hand with his free one, his voice going gentle when he said, "We'll find her, Mrs. McCloud. Hear those sirens? Two patrol cars will be pulling into your driveway any minute. We'll start a neighborhood search and put out a statewide missing child alert. We'll find her."

A sob escaped Lenore's throat and the sound of it made Deborah's chest ache. She could count on one hand the number of times she had seen her mother cry.

Three uniformed officers stepped into the open doorway, their faces as determined as Dylan's. Carefully disengaging herself from Lenore's hand, Dylan turned to them, all business now. He began to bark instructions as Deborah put an arm around her mother's waist, feeling the tremors that raced through Lenore.

Deborah suspected that at least one of the other officers outranked Dylan, but none of them were protesting his taking charge of the situation. Because his uncle was the chief of police? But even as that cynical thought crossed her mind, she knew that wasn't the explanation. People simply responded to Dylan's natural air of authority.

If it meant finding Isabelle more quickly, she wouldn't even resent him for it.

Dylan had just instructed Lenore to find recent photographs of Isabelle and had turned back to his co-workers when a cheery little voice from the stairway made them all freeze in their tracks. "Hi, Officer Smith. Did you come to find me?"

"Isabelle!" Lenore sagged against Deborah for a moment, while they all stared at the dimpled cherub at the top of the stairs.

Her pink knit pants were dirty at the knees, but other than that, Isabelle showed absolutely no sign of wear. Her golden-blond curls framed a face glowing with health, and her enormous blue eyes gleamed with what appeared to be great satisfaction.

Dylan, Lenore and Deborah all moved toward the stairs at one time. Isabelle ran down to meet them, launching herself straight toward Dylan. He caught her in mid-leap.

"You came to find me," she said, wrapping her arms around his neck. "Just like you did Benjamin. I knew you would."

Deborah's first reaction was an almost overwhelming relief that the child was unharmed. Her next thought was that she ought to turn the kid over her knee for putting them through this.

"Where were you?" Dylan asked, holding Isabelle a few inches away from him.

Looking quite pleased with herself, Isabelle replied, "In Nanna's closet."

Lenore had a hand on Isabelle's back, as if to reassure herself the child really was there. "Didn't you hear us calling you?"

Isabelle bobbed her head. "I had to put my hand on my mouth so you wouldn't hear me laughing."

A low growl escaped Deborah's throat. Ignoring Dylan's warning glance, she demanded, "What on earth were you thinking? Do you have any idea how badly you scared us?"

Looking taken aback by Deborah's anger, Isabelle blinked. "I wanted to see Officer Smith," she explained earnestly. "He came to find Benjamin when Benjamin got lost."

Dylan handed the child over to Lenore and turned to the other officers, who hovered in the doorway looking confused. "Y'all can go now," he drawled, his tone ironic. "Looks like the case is solved. I'll wrap it up here."

Tipping their hats respectfully to Lenore and Deborah, the officers left, muttering among themselves. Dylan stepped toward Deborah, lowering his voice so he wouldn't interrupt Lenore, who was scolding Isabelle even as she continued to hug her in gratitude.

"Don't be too mad at her," he murmured. "She's too young to understand exactly what she did. To her, it was just a game of hide-and-seek."

"She's old enough to know to respond when her name is called," Deborah snapped back.

Back on her feet again—and only slightly chastened by Lenore's reprimand—Isabelle moved to tug on Dylan's shirt, gazing up at him adoringly. "Nanna's got lemonade in the 'frigerator. You want some, Officer Smith?"

Not only had Isabelle not learned her lesson, she was still trying to capitalize on the situation, Deborah decided. "No, Officer Smith can't stay," she said firmly. "You dragged him here under false pretenses. You shouldn't expect to be rewarded for that."

Lenore looked reprovingly at Deborah. "Officer Smith is welcome to some lemonade after he was kind enough to come help us out."

"But—"

"Actually, I have some things to do this afternoon," Dylan cut in smoothly. "But I would like to talk with you later, if it's convenient, Mrs. McCloud."

Isabelle pouted. "You have to go now?"

Kneeling in front of her, he nodded gravely. "I'm afraid your game has cost me time that I needed to be doing other things. You know now that you shouldn't have hidden from Mrs. McCloud and Deborah, don't you?"

"But I wanted to see you," Isabelle said, her voice close to a whine. "Deborah wouldn't ask you over because she doesn't like you, but I like you and I wanted you to come visit. You found Benjamin when he was lost in the woods."

"But Benjamin really was lost," Dylan countered, notably ignoring the child's comment about Deborah not liking him. "It's my job to help people who are lost or hurt or in trouble. The way I helped you and Adrienne when you were in that car wreck a few months ago, remember?"

Isabelle nodded slowly.

"When you made up a reason to bring me here, you might have taken me away from helping someone who really needed me."

"Do you have to go help someone now?"

"Maybe. When I have lemonade with you, Isabelle, it will have to be at a time when it's convenient for everyone involved and not because of a trick you've played on us. Okay?''

Her lip quivering, Isabelle asked in a small voice, ''Are you mad at me?''

Dylan hesitated only a moment before smiling crookedly at her. ''I could never be mad at you, princess. Just promise me you won't do this again.''

She hung her head. ''Okay,'' she muttered with a heavy sigh.

Deborah grudgingly admitted that Dylan hadn't given in to Isabelle's machinations, even if he hadn't exactly been stern with her. He straightened and spoke to Lenore. ''I'll call you later to set up a time to meet with you.''

Though Lenore nodded, she added, ''But as I've already told Deborah, there's very little information I can give you. I really don't have any idea who could be, well, you know,'' she finished with a glance at Isabelle.

''I understand.'' He turned to Deborah then. ''I'll see you later.''

Because she had every intention of being in on his talk with her mother, she agreed coolly. ''Yes, you will.''

''Thank you for coming so quickly, Officer Smith,'' Lenore moved toward the door to see him out.

''Sure thing, ma'am.'' Breaking eye contact with Deborah, he took a step toward the door just as Lenore opened it.

Nathan and Caitlin stood on the other side of the door, both looking surprised that it had opened before they could ring the bell.

To say that Nathan looked surprised at finding Dylan with his mother and sister would have been an understatement. Nathan looked at Deborah with both eyebrows raised. "What's going on?"

Caitlin stepped past him before Deborah could answer, her eyes on Isabelle. "Is everything okay? Nothing's happened, I hope."

"I'll let Mrs. McCloud explain after I'm gone," Dylan said. "I'm sorry about your mother, Caitlin."

"Thank you, Dylan."

Nathan had apparently noticed that Isabelle hadn't rushed forward to meet them, but was instead lurking half-hidden behind Lenore. Even Deborah could see the guilt written on the child's angelic face—and Nathan knew Isabelle much better than Deborah did. "Just what exactly has been going on here?" he asked suspiciously.

"I'll, uh, be going now." Dylan sent Isabelle a quick, bracing smile before edging out the door. "See y'all later."

Chapter Five

It was later that evening before Dylan made it back to Lenore's house. Having called to confirm the time with her, he knew she was expecting him and that Nathan and Caitlin had already taken Isabelle home. Lenore had not mentioned the letters to Nathan, and she had reminded Dylan that she didn't want him to do so, either.

He expected that Deborah would be very much involved in his conversation with Lenore. Deborah would probably try to take charge of the whole interview, actually. She would think she was protecting her mother, but Dylan knew the real reason would be that she simply liked being in charge.

It was one of the things they had always had in common.

Deborah opened the door when Dylan rang the bell. She had changed clothes, his cop's eye noted immediately. She wore a dark-green scoop-neck T-shirt and low-slung jeans that hugged her hips and outlined her long, slender legs.

Even though he was there on business—and had reminded himself of that fact a half dozen times during the drive over—he couldn't help noticing that there was an intriguing little gap between the hem of her T-shirt and the top of her jeans. It was with some difficulty that he pulled his gaze away from that narrow expanse of creamy skin. "Evening, Ms. McCloud."

Her expression was a mixture of prickliness and impatience. "Let's just get this over with. Mother's waiting for us in the kitchen."

He motioned with one hand. "Lead the way."

He knew where the kitchen was, of course. He just wanted to watch her hips sway as she walked in front of him.

Lenore was fussing over a steaming tea kettle. A plate of homemade cookies—two different kinds—sat on the table. Lenore was obviously one of those women who cooked under stress, wearing a pearl necklace, no less.

His own mother could not have been more different from this woman.

"Do you drink tea, Officer Smith, or would you like me to make a pot of coffee?"

"Tea sounds good, ma'am. Don't go to any special trouble on my behalf."

She motioned him to a chair and brought a steaming mug to him. "Sugar?"

"Yes, ma'am. Please."

"Help yourself to some cookies. I made peanut butter and snickerdoodles."

Business, he reminded himself. But it wasn't often he got homemade cookies. He snagged a couple of them—one of each flavor—as he took his seat.

"How's Isabelle?" he asked lightly to help put the women at ease. "Did she properly learn her lesson about scaring her elders this afternoon?"

Lenore's smile was faint, but affectionate. "I'm sure she did. Nathan had a long talk with her to make sure she understood what she did wrong, and then he restricted her television viewing for the next few days to make sure she remembered the lesson."

Deborah grumbled, and Dylan got the idea she still didn't think the punishment was severe enough to be effective. The kid had really given Deborah a scare that afternoon. He knew the feeling; he'd been half-crazy with worry about the little girl.

Reminded of his reason for being there now, he pulled the letter from his pocket, laying it on the table in front of him.

Lenore's smile faded when she recognized the folded sheet of paper. She sat slowly, perching on the edge of a chair on the other side of the table from him.

He spoke first. "Deborah said you've received more than one letter like this."

He watched as she laced her fingers on the table in front of her. It was a calm, graceful pose, but he noted that her knuckles were white.

"Yes. Two, maybe three others."

"Beginning when?"

She frowned a little in concentration. "Isabelle arrived last October. I began to spend time with her in November. I believe the first letter arrived not long after Thanksgiving, perhaps the first week in December.''

''Can you remember what it said?''

Her brow furrowed a bit more deeply. ''Not the exact wording, of course. I remember that it wasn't quite as unpleasant in tone as this one. It was almost…sympathetic. Commiserating with me because Nathan brought Stuart's child to this town, telling me it was understandable that I didn't quite know how to act and offering me advice on what to do.''

''Which was?''

Lenore's chin lifted and her voice cooled by several degrees. ''It was suggested that I should publicly shun both my son and his sister, making it so unpleasant for them in this town that he would be forced to take her somewhere else. I tossed it straight into the trash, of course. To be quite honest, I thought it must be a tasteless attempt at humor.''

''Humor?'' Deborah shook her head in apparent disbelief. ''You get a threatening letter and you think it's a joke?''

''Pay attention, Deborah. I said the tone of the first letter wasn't at all threatening, merely strange.''

Dylan quickly stuffed another bite of cookie into his mouth to keep from grinning at Lenore's acerbic comment.

Having effectively chastened her daughter, Lenore turned back to Dylan. ''There was no signature and nothing about the wording of the letter to give me a clue to the writer's identity. I saw no reason to waste my time fretting, so I simply forgot about it.''

Dylan washed down the cookie with a sip of tea. ''Tell me about the second letter.''

She hesitated a few moments before answering, as

if to organize her thoughts. "It was right after Christmas. There was a holiday pageant at Isabelle's preschool, which I attended with Nathan and Caitlin, and the four of us went together to the Christmas eve program at my church. Obviously, we were seen as a family unit by quite a number of people in this town. The second letter arrived shortly after those public appearances."

"You received two creepy, anonymous letters during the holidays and you didn't say a word to any of us?" Deborah demanded.

Lenore sighed lightly. "I saw no need to do so, especially during the holidays. The boys would have gotten angry, and since we had no way of knowing who sent the letters, their anger would have accomplished nothing."

Dylan cut in quickly before Deborah could argue again. "What was the tone of the second letter?"

"Petulant," Lenore replied without a pause. "I hadn't followed the advice I'd been given. I was influencing the townspeople to accept Isabelle, by appearing in public with her as if I approved of her presence here. My actions were disillusioning to those who had been betrayed and disappointed by my husband's behavior, and a bad example for all the other wives of faithless, philandering husbands."

"So it's probably some other woman whose husband was unfaithful, right?" Deborah asked Dylan.

"Could be. Or a political supporter, possibly a financial supporter, of your father's. Someone who took his betrayal almost as personally as the family."

"Yeah. Right," Deborah muttered. Dylan wondered how many others would identify the quick flash of pain in her blue eyes.

He concentrated on Lenore to give Deborah time to mask the emotions she wouldn't want him to see. "You can't think of anyone who could be sending these letters? No one who has treated you significantly differently during the past few months? No one who has made any negative comments about Isabelle?"

Lenore took her time before answering the question. "I can't think of anyone who might have sent them," she said finally. "There were, obviously, plenty of gossips hovering around me when Nathan first brought Isabelle here, waiting to see how I would react, but no one who stands out in my mind."

She cleared her throat. "You know, I suppose, that I was initially hesitant to accept Isabelle. It was simply too painful for me, I'm ashamed to say, and I selfishly refused to have anything to do with her at first. My acquaintances all sympathized with me and agreed that Nathan had been wrong to bring Isabelle here. After my attitude changed, they took their cues from me and stopped saying anything negative about the child—at least to my face. I can't recall anyone who has continued to criticize me or Nathan since."

He nodded, having expected that answer. "What did the third letter say?"

Lenore's chin lifted a bit. "I don't know. I recognized the handwriting on the envelope and I tossed it in the trash unopened. I should have done the same with this latest one."

"When did you receive the third letter?"

"Just after Easter, I believe."

"Another family togetherness occasion," Dylan observed. "I assume you attended church together?"

"Yes, Nathan, Caitlin, Isabelle and I were in church together that morning."

"I didn't come home for Easter," Deborah murmured. "I was tied up with business."

Dylan remembered that, actually. His aunt and a few other local gossips had felt the need to comment and speculate about why Deborah McCloud hadn't come home for Easter. The general consensus at the time had been that she still resented having Isabelle at her family's holiday table, even though Deborah had behaved well enough during her Thanksgiving and Christmas visits home.

"Each letter has come after you made public appearances with Isabelle as a visible member of your family," he summarized unnecessarily, thinking aloud. "I suppose Gideon's wedding precipitated the latest one."

"Probably," Lenore agreed. "Photos of the wedding appeared in the next day's *Honesty Gazette*. There was one particularly nice shot of Isabelle and me. She was in her little flower-girl dress with a ring of flowers in her hair, and she looked adorable."

Gideon remembered that photograph, as a matter of fact. Mostly because it had been positioned next to a snapshot of Deborah with her brothers. Deborah had looked downright stunning in a form-fitting dress that had raised his blood pressure even seeing it in a grainy black-and-white newspaper photo.

Putting that image out of his mind, he looked down at the letter in front of him. "What concerns me is that the tone of the letters seems to be getting more hostile. Almost threatening."

"Because it's obvious that Mother hasn't been paying attention to them," Deborah said.

He nodded. "And probably because it's equally obvious that she not only accepts Isabelle now, but has also become quite fond of her."

"Of course I have. Anyone who spends any time around Isabelle becomes quite fond of her."

Dylan smiled in response to Lenore's indignant tone. "I'm very fond of her, myself."

He noted that Deborah didn't say anything. Was she still annoyed with Isabelle for the scare earlier, or was Deborah holding the child at an emotional distance as she seemed to do almost everyone else these days?

"You don't think there's any real threat, do you?" Lenore looked from Deborah to Dylan. "It's all just blustering, isn't it?"

"Probably. But as your daughter has pointed out, we should take a few precautions."

"Such as?"

"You should immediately report anything out of the ordinary, anything that makes you uncomfortable. Any more letters, obviously. Or unsettling phone calls. Heck, if anyone even looks at you funny, I want you to call me."

Pursing her lips, Lenore shook her head. "I doubt there will be any more letters, especially if I ignore this one and continue to appear with Isabelle in public. I mean, what can anyone hope to accomplish by a series of ugly letters, when it's obvious that I'm not being influenced by them?"

"This afternoon you were convinced that Isabelle's disappearance had something to do with the letters," Deborah reminded her. "You weren't brushing them off so lightly then."

Lenore shifted in her chair. "Yes, that was the first

thought that occurred to me. Probably because you took the letter so seriously this morning. But now that we know Isabelle was never in jeopardy, it still seems unlikely to me that anyone too cowardly to sign a letter would take the risk of actually doing anything illegal.''

Although Dylan could name entirely too many incidences in which cowards had crossed legal lines, he thought it better not to mention them at the moment. ''I would also like to speak to Nathan about this,'' he said instead.

Deborah turned abruptly in her seat to stare at him. Lenore's eyebrows drew into a deep V of disapproval. ''Why would you want to worry Nathan?''

He kept his voice gentle. ''Because someone in this town hates Isabelle. Nathan needs to be made aware of that since he is responsible for her safety.''

''I agree,'' Deborah surprised him by saying firmly. ''Nathan needs to know. After all, I'm only in town for a few more days. Someone else in the family should know what's going on.''

He couldn't help wondering if the reminder of the temporary nature of her visit was directed toward him. If so, it hadn't been necessary. Every time he saw Deborah, he was aware that she wouldn't stay.

Unaware of the silent byplay between Dylan and Deborah—at least, he supposed so—Lenore spoke again. ''I'll talk to Nathan. There's no need for you to speak with him.''

''Actually, there is. I have a few questions I'd like to ask him.''

Frustration made Lenore's sigh sound irritable. He didn't really blame her. He didn't like feeling out of control in his life, either.

"For Isabelle's sake, I think it's best if we take every reasonable precaution," he said, knowing just what button to push to ensure her cooperation.

She nodded reluctantly.

"When are you going to talk to Nathan?" Deborah demanded.

"I thought I would stop by his house after I leave here. The sooner he's put on alert, the better."

"I'll go with you."

"That won't be—"

"I'll go with you," she repeated firmly. "This is family business. You're involved only because I called you in."

"But I *am* involved now," he countered. "And it's my responsibility to—"

"I want to be there when you talk to Nathan," she cut in again.

Some things never changed—and the stubborn glint in Deborah McCloud's eyes was one of them. He knew that look well enough to be aware that no amount of arguing on his part would change her mind. The only way he could prevail was to use his authority as a police officer to bar her from his meeting with Nathan, and he wasn't sure even that would do the trick.

Because he didn't want to put it to the test just now, when it wasn't all that important, anyway, he conceded. "Okay, fine."

And then he spoke again, deliberately choosing his words to exact a bit of revenge for her pushiness. "If you want to spend more time with me, you're certainly welcome to tag along."

"I don't—" she began heatedly, and then made a

visible effort to bite off the words and reclaim her chilly tone. "Fine."

Content with his minor victory, he turned his attention back to the few remaining questions he had for Lenore.

Deborah had spent more time with Dylan in the past twelve hours than in all of the past seven years. He should have seemed almost like a stranger to her by now. After all, they had both changed a great deal since their youthful romance. Problem was, she still felt as though she knew him all too well.

She knew, for example, that he wasn't particularly happy she had insisted on accompanying him to Nathan's house. She had piqued his professional ego by defying his authority, and he had reacted with a little dig calculated to make her lose her temper and embarrass herself. At least she had avoided that scene. Barely.

They walked out of her mother's house together, though he stalked a bit ahead of her—trying to appear as if he were still in control?

"I still don't know why you're so determined to come along," he said when they were alone on her mother's front porch. "What do you think you'll accomplish that I won't?"

"I just want to hear what Nathan has to say."

He moved toward the cruiser parked in the driveway and opened the passenger-side door. "I'll bring you back home when we're finished. It shouldn't take long."

She clutched the keys she'd grabbed on her way out. "I'll follow you in my own car. You could be called away for an emergency or something."

"Not likely. I'm pretty much off duty for the rest of the evening. I told Owen I'd be looking into this letter situation, and he agreed it's something we should take seriously."

She frowned, disliking the thought of him discussing her family's business with his uncle. But that was unfair, she chided herself immediately. She was the one who had gone to him for help, precisely because he was a police officer. She had to allow him to do the job as he thought best.

Which didn't mean she intended to allow him to do so without her keeping an eye on him. "I'll follow you."

"Deborah, would you stop being a pain in the butt and get in the cruiser?" He sounded almost weary as he opened the passenger door and motioned her inside. "I know very well you aren't afraid to be alone with me. You're just being stubborn."

She was too shrewd, of course, to be taken in by clichéd reverse psychology tactics. Nor did she believe riding in her own car signified in any way that she was afraid to be alone with him. But because she didn't want to spend the next half hour arguing with him—and the look on his face let her know that was a distinct possibility—she lifted her chin and slid into the cruiser with as much dignity as she could command.

"So," he said after backing out of the driveway, "when do you go back to Tampa?"

She drew her gaze away from the interesting gadgets incorporated into the dashboard. It was her first ride in a cruiser, though she wouldn't allow herself to look too interested or impressed. "I promised

Mother I would stay until after my birthday. That's—''

"A week from tomorrow."

She turned her head to look out the passenger-door window, unsure how to respond. She knew Dylan's birthday, of course—November 29—but she was a bit disconcerted that he'd brought hers to mind so quickly. She told herself it didn't mean anything. Dylan had always had a good memory. And her twentieth birthday had been the day they had broken up, which was a fairly significant occasion for both of them, she supposed.

As for her knowing his date of birth, well, her memory wasn't so bad, either.

He chuckled unexpectedly. "Remember your eighteenth birthday? When you and I—''

She broke in brusquely. "You know what I told you earlier, when I came to your place with the letter? I said that what's going on now has nothing to do with the past. I don't want to talk about anything that happened before I came to you this afternoon."

He shrugged, his amusement gone now. "Whatever you say."

And then he spoke again, "But you can't stop me from remembering."

She had no answer for that.

Fortunately, it was a short drive to Nathan's house. Deborah was relieved when Dylan turned into the driveway. She didn't wait for him to walk around and open her door. She was out of the cruiser almost before he turned off the engine.

Nathan answered the door when Deborah pushed the bell. His eyebrows shot up in surprise when he saw Deborah and Dylan on his doorstep. And then they drew downward into a frown of concern. "What's wrong?"

"Mother's fine," Deborah assured him quickly.

"Gideon?"

"Gideon's fine, too. Nothing's happened, Nathan, we're just here to discuss something with you."

Relief made his shoulders sag a moment. "You gave me a scare," he admitted. "For some reason, my mind leaped straight to the worst-case scenario. Guess I'm just tired."

"We won't take much of your time," Dylan assured him, stepping up beside Deborah. "We just need to talk to you about something."

"Oh?" His eyebrows rose again, and this time there was a glint of familiar mischief in his eyes. He gestured between them with one hand. "So, are the two of you…?"

"No!" Deborah snapped, feeling her face go hot.

"I'm here in an official capacity," Dylan said, avoiding Deborah's eyes. "Deborah is here because it involves your family."

"Come in." Nathan closed the front door behind them. "Does this have anything to do with Isabelle's crazy stunt this afternoon? Caitlin and I have both talked to her about what she did."

Dylan shook his head. "No, though it does concern Isabelle. Is Caitlin here? She might want to join us."

"Caitlin's tucking Isabelle into bed."

"I'm here." Overhearing her husband's words, Caitlin stepped into the living room where Nathan had led their unexpected guests. "What's going on?"

Dylan waited until everyone was seated—Nathan and Caitlin together on a deep sofa, Deborah and

Dylan in matching wingback chairs. He then gave Nathan and Caitlin a concise explanation of everything he had learned since Deborah appeared at his door earlier that afternoon, including reading them the letter Deborah had brought with her.

By the time he'd finished speaking, Nathan and Caitlin were looking at each other in a way that made Deborah ask, "Why don't you look more surprised?"

"Because," Nathan answered, his face set in grim lines, "I've gotten anonymous letters, too."

Chapter Six

"*What?*" Deborah stared at her brother and sister-in-law in disbelief. "You've gotten letters like this and you didn't mention them? Not even when you went out of town and left Isabelle in Mother's care?"

"I didn't see any real threat." Nathan sounded uncharacteristically defensive. "I only got a couple of anonymous letters, both of them before Christmas. I didn't expect any further deliveries, and I certainly had no idea someone was also writing to Mom."

Dylan had switched instantly into no-nonsense-cop mode, Deborah noted. "You said you received two letters? Both unsigned?"

"That's correct."

"But nothing since Christmas."

"Also correct."

"I don't suppose you kept them."

"Actually, I did. I'm an attorney," Nathan added. "I keep everything."

"Do you mind if I see them?"

"You'll have to come to the office tomorrow. I keep them there."

"Then Irene must have seen them," Deborah surmised. "Nothing escapes your scary office manager."

"I've shown the letters to no one except Caitlin," Nathan corrected her. "I have one drawer in my office for confidential papers. Irene would never dream of looking in there. That's where I filed the letters. I figured I would hang onto them for a year or so, then get rid of them if I heard nothing more."

"You never considered calling the police?" Dylan inquired.

Dylan was probably no more surprised than Deborah when Nathan smiled a little and shook his head. "I saw no reason to involve the police in my affairs, especially when no specific threat had been made against me or anyone in my family."

Deborah watched Caitlin and Dylan exchange an ironic glance. "The McCloud pride," Caitlin murmured.

"Formidable, isn't it?" Dylan replied, breaking out of professional mode long enough to flash Caitlin a wry smile.

"Stubborn," Caitlin agreed.

"Very."

"Did we suddenly become invisible?" Nathan asked Deborah.

She was not amused.

All business again, Dylan turned his attention back to Nathan. "When did you receive the first letter?"

"A couple of days after Thanksgiving. It came here to the house, unsigned, no return address. The writer called me every bad name but cannibal for bringing Isabelle here and said she was a slap in the face to every decent, honest, moral, responsible citizen of this town."

"And yet there were no threats, either direct or implied?"

"No. Just dire predictions that I would become a pariah in the town. That my own family would reject me and I would grow to regret making such a foolish and selfish decision. I wrote it off as the ramblings of some nutcase busybody. After all, I had just gotten engaged to the love of my life—" he shot a dazzling smile toward Caitlin before continuing "—and I had had a nice Thanksgiving dinner with my family, at which Isabelle had been welcomed. I knew the letter-writer was completely off-base."

"And the second letter?"

"That one arrived a couple of weeks later, just before Christmas. The announcement of our engagement had just made the papers, and we were busy with holiday programs and preparations. The letter said pretty much the same things as the first one. I almost crumpled it up and tossed it in the trash, but I filed it with the other in case I needed them. When no more letters arrived, I assumed the nut had given up and gone away."

"And you didn't think you should mention those letters to anyone else in the family?" Deborah asked.

Nathan shrugged. "I told you, I didn't take them seriously. Caitlin and I keep a close watch on Isabelle, anyway, but there was no threat to her in the letters. Just tirades about my insensitivity and poor judgment. I saw no need to worry Mom.''

"So you let her worry all by herself.''

"I didn't know she was getting letters, too! How could I have known?''

"You could have asked.''

"Oh, sure, right. 'Hey, Mom, has anyone been sending you bizarre letters lately?' ''

"If you had told her about your letters, she would have—''

"Dylan, would you like a cup of tea?'' Caitlin asked, her voice raised over Deborah's. "This could go on for a while.''

Dylan smiled and stood. "No, thank you. I'd better be going. Nathan, I'll stop by your office sometime tomorrow, if that's convenient. In the meantime, maybe you could be thinking of a list of potential suspects.''

"I'll try,'' Nathan agreed, letting the argument with Deborah drop. "But I can't come up with any-one weird enough—well, yeah, I guess I can—but I still don't have a clue who might have sent those letters.''

"What I don't understand,'' Caitlin mused as she rose with the others, "is why whoever it is keeps writing to Lenore. Nathan and I are the ones who have Isabelle.''

Dylan nodded. "Apparently, whoever it is knows that you and Nathan can't be swayed where Isabelle is concerned. Nathan's never been particularly wor-ried about what anyone else thought of him, anyway, with the exception of his family, of course. Lenore appears, at least outwardly, to be more concerned with her social status. And since everyone knows she was initially resistant to Isabelle, perhaps the letter writer thought there was still a chance to convince Lenore to withhold her approval. First through sympathy, and then through intimidation. Obviously, whoever it is doesn't know your mother very well at all.''

Deborah wouldn't have thought Dylan would know her family particularly well, either. Yet he had just neatly summed up both Nathan and Lenore. She couldn't help wondering just how well he still knew *her*.

Making a courteous exit, Dylan reminded both Nathan and Caitlin to let him know if anything out of the ordinary occurred.

''We will,'' Caitlin replied, seeing them off. ''It was nice having you here, Dylan. Maybe you can come back under more pleasant circumstances soon.''

Deborah watched as Dylan gave her sister-in-law one of his almost irresistible, lazy-cowboy smiles. ''I'd like that, ma'am,'' he drawled.

Deborah turned on one heel with an impatient mutter. The last thing she had ever intended when she went to Dylan for advice that afternoon was to bring him into her family circle.

She stalked toward the cruiser with a heavy scowl specifically designed to hide any clue that after all these years, she still wasn't entirely immune to Dylan Smith's smiles.

''So, what do you think?'' Deborah asked as soon as they were on the road again.

Dylan glanced at her before returning his attention to his driving. ''About what?''

"About the letters Nathan received, of course."

"Oh. Most likely, the same person who wrote to your mother sent the letters to your brother."

Deborah rolled her eyes. "*I* could have said that. Is this an example of your brilliant police work?"

"What do you want me to say, Deb? I have no better idea than you do of who wrote the letters. Being a cop doesn't make me a psychic."

The familiar shortening of her name made her scowl, as did his curt tone. "So what *are* you going to do next?"

"There's really not much I can do at this point. With no evidence of who sent the letters and nothing that's actually happened otherwise, I have no real leads to pursue. All I can do is some discreet snooping, tap into the grapevine to see who's done the most mouthing about Isabelle. Of course, chances are the person hasn't said anything to anyone. Anonymous complainers tend to be too cowardly to speak up."

She wasn't satisfied, but she had to acknowledge that there was really nothing more he could do. At least now she knew Nathan was also on alert, which would be a great relief to her when she left next week. Nathan would do anything necessary to protect his family.

"I'll do everything I can, Deb," Dylan assured her quietly. "But there's probably nothing to worry about. I agree with Nathan that it's probably just a nut with nothing better to do."

"I hope you're right." Deborah remembered the look on Lenore's face that morning. "No one has the right to try to bully my mother this way. Whether she chooses to act as a surrogate grandmother to Isabelle is no one's business but her own."

"I doubt that it's anyone who knows your family well or spends much time around them. I can't imagine anyone who could meet your little sister and not fall for her. She's just about the cutest kid I've ever known."

"I haven't spent a lot of time around kids, including this one, but I agree that Isabelle's very bright and generally well-behaved. Her stunt today was unusual for her. I hope it's not a forewarning of things to come."

"I'm sure it's not. She was just using four-year-old logic to get what she wanted. Her friend Benjamin got lots of attention when he disappeared for a few hours, so it made sense to her to do the same thing. I have a feeling your brother has made it clear to her that she can't get away with anything like that in the future."

"I certainly hope so. She scared my poor mother half to death."

"She scared me, too," Dylan admitted. "I didn't want to think that anything might have happened to her. We don't get a lot of violent crime in this town, of course, but I've seen enough to dread what we might have found."

"Anyone who watches television or reads the newspapers knows what could have happened." Deborah shuddered just thinking about some of the horrific news reports of the past few years. "I don't know how anyone has the courage even to have kids these days."

He waited a beat before responding. "That's your new credo? If you don't get attached, you don't get hurt?"

Even she heard the defensiveness in her tone when she snapped, "I didn't say that."

"Not in so many words. But that's the way you've lived for the past few years, isn't it? Always on the move, no roots or strings."

She crossed her arms over her chest, gripping her forearms tightly. "Been keeping tabs on my movements, officer?"

"In this town, everyone keeps tabs. And reports them to everyone else," he added lightly. "That's why I said I'm going to rely on the local grapevine to find some clues as to who wrote the letters."

"Yes, well, confine your snooping to that issue and leave my movements out of it."

"No problem." His voice was as hard as his face now. "I do have plenty of other things to do."

He turned the cruiser into her mother's driveway and braked hard enough to make her seatbelt tighten momentarily around her. She had made him angry. And she knew she had done so deliberately because she was more comfortable with him as an adversary than as a partner in solving her family problems.

Don't get attached. Don't get hurt again.

It annoyed her even further that his words seemed so fitting to the way she felt—now and for the past seven years.

She reached for the door handle. "You'll let me know if you come up with anything about the letter-writer's identity?"

"Of course. And I assume you'll contact me if anything else happens to concern any of you."

"Yes. Um, thanks for helping us out."

"It's my job."

Nodding, she opened the door and turned toward it.

His right hand fell on her left arm, holding her in her seat for a moment. "Deb?"

"Yes?" she asked without looking around at him.

"I'm glad you trusted me enough to come to me."

She swallowed before answering. "As you said, it's your job."

Sliding out of his light clasp, she exited the car and closed the door behind her. She didn't look back as she hurried toward the front door of her mother's house.

Lindsey Newman returned from her brief sales trip on Tuesday and called Deborah that evening. "I heard there was some excitement at your place yesterday. Three police cars in your driveway, another in Nathan's driveway last night."

Deborah stared at the receiver for a moment as if she could study Lindsey's gamine face through the phone lines. "How could you have heard about that already?"

"I stopped for gas at the Kwickee Market on Hill Street. Edna Cunningham told me she heard all about it from Lucille Mayo, your mom's next-door neighbor. Lucille told Edna that Isabelle went missing for a time, but turned up unharmed."

Lenore's neighbors had all called, of course, to find out about the police cars, but Deborah hadn't realized the news would have spread quite this quickly. She had almost forgotten the efficiency of the Honesty grapevine, though she remembered how avidly it had buzzed during the scandal her father had created.

"Isabelle's fine," she said to distract herself from

that memory. "We just misplaced her for a short time."

Chuckling at Deborah's wording, Lindsey changed the subject. "Have you had a chance to look over the material I left with you?"

"Yes, though I'm afraid I haven't had enough time to make a decision." Between Isabelle's stunt, worrying about the anonymous letters and spending most of last night trying not to think about Dylan, Deborah had actually given very little thought to Lindsey's business proposition during the past thirty-six hours.

"I understand. Maybe you'd like to get together again tomorrow to talk about it some more?"

"Sure. Why not?" Though Deborah still doubted that she would be interested in going into business here with Lindsey, she figured it wouldn't hurt to discuss the possibility.

"Lunch? We can meet at Casa Familia. It's quiet there, and we can talk as long as we want without getting evil eyes from impatient wait staff."

Deborah smiled. "You're on. What time?"

"I have a few things to do in the morning. One o'clock?"

"See you then."

Dylan wasn't actually keeping a watch for Deborah's car, but her silver-blue two-seater was hard to miss in this relatively small town. He caught a glimpse of it as he drove the cruiser past Casa Familia early Tuesday afternoon. It was purely instinct that made him turn the cruiser into the parking lot.

It occurred to him as he climbed out of the car that some people might think his behavior questionable. Deliberately putting himself in the same places as

Deborah, when he was the last person on earth she wanted to see, could be construed as a bit strange. Masochistic, at the least.

And yet he found himself pushing through the heavy glass door that led into the restaurant, already searching the dining room for Deborah.

A dark-haired, brown-skinned, middle-aged man with gleaming dark eyes and a blindingly white smile beneath a neat mustache greeted Dylan when he walked in. The man's accent was as Southern as Dylan's own when he drawled a welcome. "Hey, Officer Smith. Been a while since you've been in."

"Hey, Bob. How's it going?"

"Can't complain. You?"

"Not bad." Dylan discreetly scanned the room again. There weren't many customers now that the lunch rush was past, and the ones left were seated at comfortable distances. Deborah's golden hair gleamed in the intimately dim lighting, drawing his gaze to the table in the back corner where she sat with someone else.

It took him a moment to identify the other woman because her back was partially turned to him. And then she made an expressive, very recognizable gesture with one hand, followed by a throaty laugh that drifted across the room to him. Lindsey Newman. An old schoolmate. He knew Lindsey was a good friend of Deborah's sister-in-law, Caitlin, but he hadn't realized Lindsey and Deborah were pals.

"Sit anywhere you like," Bob encouraged him. "Plenty of tables available now."

"Thanks." Dylan headed straight toward the back of the dining room.

Lindsey paused in her rapid talking when Dylan stopped beside the table. "Oh. Hello."

"Lindsey." He nodded politely at the more-cute-than-pretty redhead, then glanced at her companion. "Hi, Deborah."

She glared at him. "Are you following me, Smith?"

He smiled. "Nope."

Taking advantage of every coincidental encounter, perhaps, but he wasn't following her.

Lindsey and Deborah had apparently been there just long enough to get a good start on their lunches—a large taco salad for Lindsey, chicken enchiladas for Deborah. Half-empty bowls of tortilla chips and cheese dip sat between them. A thick red folder bulging with papers lay on the far edge of the table. Curiosity nagged him, but he kept his smile bland.

"I've had a busy morning. First day back on day shift," he said. "Two rush-hour fender benders, a car stolen from a used-car lot during the night, a fight over at the junior high. I'm just now getting a break for lunch."

"Why don't you join us?" Lindsey motioned cheerily toward one of the two empty chairs at the table for four. "I would just love to hear all about the fight at the junior high. Was it teachers or students?"

The look Deborah gave her dining companion could best be described as scorching. "I thought we had some things to discuss?"

"We can talk about them later," Lindsey replied with a careless wave on one hand. "It would be impolite to make poor Officer Smith eat alone after his trying morning, wouldn't it?''

Deborah's expression made it clear that she was prepared to be a lot ruder. She was prevented from doing so by the arrival of a dark-haired young waiter whom Dylan recognized as Bob Sanchez's eldest son.

''Hi, Officer Smith. You need a table?''

''He'll be joining us,'' Lindsey said, earning herself another look from Deborah. ''Bring the man some chips and dip. He looks hungry.''

''I'll have a fiesta platter and iced tea,'' Dylan added, pulling up one of the chairs. He knew he would pay for this later—Deborah's irritation was almost palpable—but he couldn't resist.

After all, he rationalized, it would be rude to turn down Lindsey's courteous invitation.

''How's the fishing-lure business, Lindsey?'' he asked.

''Oh, we just keep reeling in customers,'' she quipped in return, making him grin. ''Tell us about the school fight.''

He shrugged. ''Two knucklehead boys got into a fight over some cheerleader who had probably been leading them both on. Several of their pals jumped into the action and fists and books and chairs started flying. By the time Roy and I arrived, it was pretty much over. The principal and teachers had regained control.''

''Kids are so wild these days,'' Lindsey mused. ''All those violent movies and video games, I guess.''

''Most kids are still pretty decent, from my experience,'' Dylan replied. ''The ones who aren't, well, the media's only part of the problem. It comes down to poor parenting in most cases. No discipline, no firm limits, no supervision.''

He had just pretty much described his own childhood prior to being taken in by his uncle, whose parenting methods were exactly opposite to what he had just described. "I was pretty wild myself in junior high," he added wryly. "Got hauled to the principal's office more times than I can remember.''

"Then there must be hope for the knuckleheads yet," Lindsey said with a smile. "You certainly turned out very well.''

Dylan waited a beat for Deborah to make a sarcastic comment. When she only ignored him and took a bite of her enchilada, he replied to Lindsey, "Thanks. I give a lot of credit to my aunt and uncle. They took me in when I was fifteen and drilled some common sense into my hard head.''

Deborah muttered something then, but he didn't catch what she said.

"I beg your pardon?''

"Nothing," she said, not meeting his eyes as she reached for her glass of fruit punch.

"So when did you and Deborah start dating?'' Lindsey's expression was that of a kitten who strolls boldly into a lion's den.

Deborah choked on a sip of punch.

Dylan waited until his food had been placed in front of him before answering Lindsey's reckless question. Deborah started to say something, probably in an attempt to change the subject, but he spoke over her. "Deborah and I started dating when she had just turned sixteen and I was nineteen. We broke up on her twentieth birthday.''

Lindsey looked from Dylan to Deborah. "So you were just kids, basically."

He kept his eyes on his plate. "Yeah. Just kids."

But the heartache had been fully adult-sized, he could have added. And it had lasted a very long time.

"Well, there you go. No reason you can't be friendly now." Lindsey beamed at them. "Heck, I'm still buddies with all my old boyfriends."

"Deborah and I are quite friendly." Dylan smiled at Deborah as he spoke, daring her to contradict him. "Her insults and sarcastic remarks to me are merely indications that she's comfortable enough with me not to have to be pleasant and polite in my presence."

"Oh, is that what it is?" Lindsey sounded amused by his reasoning. "I'm glad to know she doesn't really dislike you as much as she pretends."

When Deborah still didn't comment, Dylan figured she must be biting her tongue hard enough to draw blood. Taking pity on her, he changed the subject. "So, are you two just having a catch-up lunch while Deborah's in town?"

"Actually—ouch." Lindsey frowned across the table at Deborah, then said to Dylan, "Yes, that's it. Just a friendly lunch."

It was quite obvious that Lindsey had just been kicked beneath the table, probably hard enough to cause a limp. Whatever the reason for their meeting, Deborah didn't want to discuss it with him.

No problem. He figured he would find out soon enough. "It's nice that you had a chance to get together," he said, pretending he hadn't noticed anything out of the ordinary.

Had it been up to Deborah, there might have been

a long, awkward silence then. Lindsey didn't believe in long pauses. She chattered nonstop as they finished their lunches, barely giving Dylan time to respond before moving on to the next topic.

Finally, pausing for breath, Lindsey dropped her napkin beside her nearly empty plate. ''I'll be back in a few,'' she said and headed for the back of the restaurant where a sign pointed the way to the rest rooms.

Deborah and Dylan were left to stare at each other across the small table, alone together once again.

Chapter Seven

All too conscious of the silence between Deborah and himself, Dylan drained the last of his coffee before bringing up the one topic he knew she would respond to. "I stopped by Nathan's office earlier, got copies of the two letters he received."

Sure enough, that got her attention. "What did they say?"

"They were similar to the one you brought me, only more hostile. As Nathan told us, he was called a long list of unflattering names, including traitor and heartless son, and pretty much ordered to pack up Isabelle and leave town."

Dylan watched as temper glinted in Deborah's blue eyes, and he knew she was furious all over again that anyone dared to give orders to any member of her family. "Do you have any leads yet?"

He shook his head. "No. But I'm still asking around."

"Is that why you followed me here? To give me an update?"

"I did not follow you here. I have a life, Deb. A busy one."

She looked at him skeptically.

He gave a gusty sigh. "I saw your car in the parking lot, okay? I was on my way to grab a deli sandwich or something and I decided to have Mexican, instead. I wasn't following you, but I came in when I saw that you were here."

"Why?"

Making a face, he shrugged. "I've recently reached the conclusion that I have a previously unsuspected streak of masochism."

"What do you mean by—"

Returning to the table then, Lindsey slid back into her seat. "Did I miss anything juicy?"

"Not at all," Deborah replied.

"Good. So, Dylan, what's this I hear about you being Honesty's next best-selling author?"

Dylan dropped the napkin he'd just taken from his lap. He glanced at Deborah as he retrieved it, noting that she still looked annoyed, but not surprised. Which meant, he concluded, that she had already known. "How did you hear that?" he asked Lindsey.

"I have my sources," she replied with what she probably fancied was a mysterious smile. "It's true, isn't it? You've written a book?"

"Yeah, it's true," he admitted reluctantly, since this wasn't a subject he was prepared to discuss.

"Cool. Is Adrienne going to represent you?"

He shifted in his seat, risking another glance at

Deborah. "Yes. She's already sent it out to a couple of editors."

"Tell us more," Lindsey encouraged. "What's your book about? How long have you been working on it? When did you decide you wanted to write a book?"

Thinking that this would be a very good time for his radio to squawk, Dylan glanced at his watch. "I really have to get back to work soon. Maybe we could talk about this another time?"

The smile Lindsey gave him then could only be described as flirtatious. "That sounds good to me. I would love to hear all about it—any time you want to tell me."

If that was a not-so-subtle hint that she would be willing to go out with him sometime, he only wished he were interested. Lindsey was certainly attractive with her tumbled red hair, wide-set green eyes and a mouth that was almost incongruously sexy in contrast with her wholesome image. She was good company, if a bit hyper. Dylan was sure many men would be delighted to take her up on her implied offer. Which made him a certified idiot for being much more interested in the blonde sitting across the table glaring at him.

Tossing his napkin on the table beside his well-cleaned plate, he stood. "Thanks for inviting me to join you, ladies. It was a pleasure."

"Any time," Lindsey returned. "Right, Deborah?"

Deborah nodded. "See you around, Dylan."

He would make sure of that.

Deborah waited until Dylan was all the way out of the restaurant before she leaned toward Lindsey.

"What was that all about?"

Lindsey didn't do bemused innocence very well, though she certainly gave it a try. "What was what all about?"

"Dylan, that's what! Asking him to join us, grilling him about his past relationship with me, snooping into his personal business—and then practically crawling into his lap flirting with him."

"Jealous?"

"*No*, I'm not—" Seeing the mischief in Lindsey's eyes, Deborah brought herself up short. "Are you trying to make an enemy of me?" she asked more mildly.

"Of course not. I'm trying to make a business partner out of you."

"Then why—?"

"I couldn't resist," Lindsey admitted. "He looked like the new kid on the playground, hoping someone would invite him to play."

Picturing Dylan's rugged, rough-cut, decidedly *un*-boyish features, Deborah found Lindsey's analogy hard to believe.

"As for asking about the past, well, I always think it's better to acknowledge the gorilla in the drawing room than to pretend he isn't there."

Deborah shook her head. "I don't even know what that was supposed to mean."

"We all know the two of you used to date. Pretending you didn't just makes things awkward. Acknowledging it and moving on makes the conversation so much more comfortable, don't you think?"

"No, I—"

"The same with his book. *You* know he's written

one, *I* know he's written one, he certainly knows—
might as well get it out in the open. As for flirting—
heck, I just like to flirt. Dylan's single and sexy as
all get-out. If he was inclined to ask me out, I'd certainly be inclined to accept. Not that I expect that to
happen, of course.''

''I don't know why not,'' Deborah grumbled. She
found it all too easy to picture Dylan and Lindsey
together. And the mental image made her stomach
ache, a reaction she tried and failed to attribute to her
hearty Mexican meal.

Lindsey laughed softly, ''I would explain why not,
but since I'd rather have you as a business partner
than an enemy, I'll let it pass.''

''You just delight in talking in riddles, don't
you?''

''Actually, I would rather talk numbers.'' Her attitude taking a complete turnaround, Lindsey reached
for the folder. ''I've got some sales and expense projections here that a CPA friend of mine put together
for us. We should take a few minutes to go over them
while we're here.''

Though she was no more convinced that she was
interested in Lindsey's business proposition now than
she had been before, Deborah turned her attention
willingly enough to the figures. After all, numbers
were a much safer subject than Dylan Smith.

It was a noisy scene around Owen and Myra
Smith's dining-room table Wednesday evening. This
family believed that good food was best enjoyed
with lively conversation, even the occasional spirited
debate. As Dylan chewed a mouthful of his aunt

Myra's pot roast, it occurred to him that Lindsey would fit in very well with his family.

If he had any sense at all, he would ask her out. As his aunt reminded him at every opportunity, it was time to be thinking about settling down. Having a family of his own. Lindsey would undoubtedly make a terrific wife and mother.

Just not with him.

His uncle, the stocky, balding, sun-weathered police chief, sat at the head of the table, arguing foreign policy with one of his sons-in-law, Mark Potter, a general medicine practitioner. Mark's wife, Gail, was wiping gravy from the chin of their youngest child, six-year-old Andrew, while their eight-year-old, Andrea, chattered with Grandma Myra.

Gail's sister Amy sat directly across the table from Dylan, her husband Curtis at her side. They were engaged in a discussion with the youngest Smith sister, thirty-two-year-old Eileen. From what Dylan overheard, they were dissecting a recent blockbuster movie that Curtis had liked, Amy hated and Eileen remained neutral about.

A portable crib had been set up at one end of the table. Five-week-old Daniel Rowlett, son of Amy and Curtis, snoozed inside it, happily oblivious that he was the guest of honor at this gathering. The Rowletts lived in Baton Rouge, Louisiana, and had arrived in Honesty that afternoon to introduce their son to the members of the family who hadn't yet met him.

Dylan had been an integral part of this family since he was fifteen, and never once had he been made to feel like an outsider. Gail, Amy and Eileen, a trio of gray-eyed brunettes who all bore a strong family resemblance to him, had treated him more like a kid brother than a cousin. They had welcomed him even when he had arrived rebellious, undisciplined and angry that he'd been taken away from the wild, unrestricted life he'd been drifting into and placed under the close supervision of his drill sergeant of an uncle.

Owen's sister Nora had never married her son's father, nor even stayed in contact with the man, and motherhood had never been high on her list of priorities. Dylan hadn't even realized how much he'd craved parental guidance until Owen and Myra had opened their home and hearts to him.

Munching on a broccoli floret, Dylan turned his gaze to the head of the table, where Owen seemed to be winning the political argument with his son-in-law. Dylan wasn't surprised, of course. Owen rarely lost. He had certainly triumphed in the fierce battle of wills with his defiant teenage nephew, earning Dylan's lifelong respect and affection in the process.

Owen was, quite frankly, Dylan's hero. Dylan considered his uncle to be the finest, most honorable man he had ever known. He couldn't imagine how he would feel if Owen were suddenly revealed to have deep character flaws, or if Owen were to do something that would devastate this happy and secure family.

Imagining that scenario was as close as Dylan could come to understanding how Deborah must have felt when the father she had idolized had broken her family's hearts.

"You're being awfully quiet, Dylan," Amy observed, turning her attention to him for a moment. "Is everything okay?"

"I'm fine," he assured her. "Just enjoying this

excellent meal. You outdid yourself this evening, Aunt Myra.''

His plump, salt-and-pepper-haired aunt preened. ''Thank you, dear. Would you like some more potatoes?''

''No, thanks. I'm saving room for your coconut pie.''

Gail looked over her son's head to speak to Amy. ''Bet I know what has Dylan so distracted. Did you know Deborah McCloud's in town?''

''Oh?'' Both Amy and Eileen turned to look speculatively at Dylan.

''I heard they've been seen around town together a couple of times,'' Gail added, and now everyone was looking at Dylan.

''Are you seeing Deborah again, Dylan?'' Amy asked.

''Who's Deborah?'' Curtis, who had been a member of the family less than two years, wanted to know.

''I've told you about her,'' Amy stage-whispered. ''His old girlfriend.''

''Oh, yeah. The one who—''

Amy cleared her throat loudly, giving her husband a warning look that caused him to fall silent.

''Deborah and I are not seeing each other again,'' Dylan said flatly. ''We ran into each other by accident a couple of times, and she came to me to ask my advice as a police officer about something that concerned her mother. That's the extent of it.''

''So maybe if she moves back to town you'll ask her out again?'' Gail hinted broadly.

''She's not moving back to Honesty. She's only here for an extended visit with her family.''

"She'll move here if she goes into business with Lindsey Newman," Gail countered.

"Deborah and Lindsey are going into business together?" Myra asked with interest.

Gail shrugged. "I think it's up to Deborah. Lindsey's been talking about some sort of business franchise she wants to open and she's asked Deborah to be a partner in it. Lindsey told Carolyn—you know, the CPA who does Mark's taxes?—that she's going to open the business even if Deborah's not interested. She'll just have to find someone else to go in on it with her."

Dylan remembered the thick red folder he'd seen on the table yesterday when he had joined Lindsey and Deborah for lunch. Now he knew it must have been a business proposal. And it was obvious that Deborah hadn't wanted him to know about it.

He tried to imagine having Deborah in town again. All the time. Running into her the way he had the past few days, never knowing when he might see her. Hearing about everything she did from the friendly gossips in town.

After their breakup, he had left Honesty to work in New Orleans for several years just so he *wouldn't* have to hear about Deborah all the time. He'd moved back a few years ago to prove to himself that he was over her and because he refused to allow the bad memories to keep him away from his family.

He had been in New Orleans when he'd heard the news about Deborah's father abandoning the family for his pregnant girlfriend. Even then his first impulse had been to run to her, to offer comfort. Dylan had disliked Stuart McCloud intensely, but Deborah had adored him, which had been a big part of the reason she and Dylan broke up. He'd known how shattered she must have been by her father's betrayal and the humiliating scandal that had followed. He had known as well that he would be the very last person she would have wanted to see during that debacle.

"Well, I think you should ask her out again," Gail proclaimed. "You and Deborah always made such an attractive couple. And you're not getting any younger, you know."

Eileen sighed gustily. "Leave him alone, Gail. You sound just like Mother. I'm thirty-two, and you don't see me rushing to marry the first guy who comes along."

"Wouldn't hurt you to think about it, either," her eldest sister retorted. "Your biological clock is running low on batteries, you know."

Eileen snorted. "That's the most ridiculous thing I've ever heard. And, anyway, I don't think Deborah McCloud is right for Dylan at all. She's entirely too spoiled and self-centered. And cold enough for ice to freeze on her—"

"Eileen!" Gail cut in hastily, casting a warning glance at her children, who were listening with interest to the adult conversation. "That's not a nice way to talk about someone. And I always liked Deborah. She's independent and self-confident, a woman who knows her own mind and is perfectly capable of providing for herself. Yet she loves her family and has stayed in close contact with her mother."

"She didn't even come home for Easter," Eileen argued. "Lucille Mayo said she would bet it's because of that little girl. Deborah didn't want Nathan to bring her here. Probably doesn't like sharing attention with another little sister."

"That's unlikely," Myra piped in. "The family seems very fond of little Isabella. Deborah even took her to a movie last weekend. Carlene Jefferson was there with her granddaughters and saw them herself."

"The child's name is Isabelle, and Deborah gets along fine with her," Dylan said, then made an attempt to change the subject. "Did anyone see the six o'clock news this evening? Seems there was a—"

"I sort of agree with Eileen," Amy interrupted as if Dylan weren't making a sound. "Not about Deborah, exactly—I always liked her well enough. I just don't think she and Dylan are particularly good together. Remember how unhappy he was when things started going badly for them? And how much he suffered when they broke up? I would hate to see him get hurt like that again."

"Would you women stop talking about Dylan as if he weren't even at the table?" Owen said in exasperation. "For Pete's sake."

"*Thank* you," Dylan said.

"So, Dylan, you following the NASCAR points race?" Mark asked blandly. At the same time, little Daniel stirred and whimpered in his crib, drawing the women's attention.

Dylan smiled. The guys were rallying to his aid now, and he greatly appreciated it. He did not want to talk about Deborah—past, present, or future—with his well-meaning but meddlesome family.

Deborah and Lenore made an hour-and-a-half drive to a large outlet mall Friday morning. They spent the day shopping for bargains, lunching at a chain steakhouse located next to the mall and then returning for another couple of hours to scour the stores they hadn't visited yet. It was the first time they had been shopping together in ages, and both enjoyed it, spending too much time dawdling over sale racks and too much money on impulse purchases.

Deborah was almost surprised by how much fun she had that day. It was nice to be away from Honesty, leaving the troubling letters and family complications behind her. Not to mention that there was almost no chance she would run into Dylan at an outlet mall.

As much as she liked being with her brothers and their wives, it was nice having Lenore all to herself. Even if Lenore did seem inclined to buy more things for Isabelle than for herself, making it impossible for Deborah to put the child out of her mind for long.

Deborah listened with resigned patience as her mother engaged in conversation with a woman buying clothes for her two young granddaughters at a popular children's clothing store. Lenore boasted a bit about Isabelle's cleverness and beauty while she filled Deborah's arms with purchases for the child. Lenore acted for all the world like a doting grandmother, even pulling out photographs of Isabelle when the other woman produced pictures of her own. Each of them made polite noises of admiration over the other's photographs, but it was obvious that they both walked away thinking their own little girls were by far the most appealing.

Deborah had become accustomed for the most part to her mother's fondness for Isabelle. Yet there were still times when she found herself bemused by Lenore's proud-grandma attitude. She couldn't really blame other people for finding the relationship odd enough to invoke a bit of gossip.

Not that any of that excused the fruitcake who had been writing those eerie letters.

"Do you really think Isabelle needs all these clothes?" Deborah asked her mother to push that unwelcome thought out of her mind. "You've got an entire wardrobe here and that doesn't count the things you've already bought today."

Lenore had the grace to look momentarily sheepish, but then she shrugged. "Isabelle doesn't have many things for summer. She's outgrown everything from last year, and besides, she didn't bring much with her when Nathan brought her here from California last fall."

"Yes, but both Nathan and Caitlin are successful attorneys. I'm sure they can afford to buy clothes for their ward."

"Of course they can. But they're busy and they don't have much time to shop. Besides, I enjoy buying things for Isabelle. It's been a long time since I've had a little girl to shop for." Lenore gave Deborah a somewhat nostalgic smile. "She does look so much like you did at that age."

Deborah wondered if that resemblance made it easier for Lenore to accept Isabelle. Perhaps it gave her a sense of connection to the child who was in no way related to her, except through a growing bond of love.

While Deborah wasn't jealous of her family's attachment to the newest member of their clan, she did envy their ability to put the past behind them and move on. Even Gideon seemed to have made some sort of peace within himself about their father, and he had been the one who had always struggled with his complicated and stormy relationship with Stuart.

Deborah herself was still having trouble looking at Isabelle without remembering the pain the child's conception had caused. While she knew that wasn't fair to the little girl, it was a daily struggle for Deborah, one that she would be glad to leave behind her when she ran away from Honesty again.

Frowning, she immediately mentally corrected herself for that thought. She wasn't running away from Honesty, she assured herself. Not even from the memories. She simply preferred to seek her future elsewhere, for many reasons.

It would have been nice if she'd felt a bit more confident in her self-assurances.

It took several trips to carry all the bags and packages from the car into Lenore's kitchen later that afternoon. Deborah piled the last of the purchases onto the kitchen table with a sigh of relief.

"I knew we'd bought a lot, but not quite this much." She turned to her mother, who had been standing at the counter leafing through the bills and advertisements that made up a typical mail delivery. "We found some pretty good—what's wrong?"

Deborah was afraid she already knew the answer to the abrupt question. Lenore confirmed her fear by wordlessly holding out an unopened envelope.

A feeling of dread flooded through Deborah, crowding out the pleasantly weary aftereffects of the shopping excursion. "Is that—"

Lenore nodded. "I recognize the handwriting."

"Are you going to open it?"

"Maybe we should call Dylan first."

Deborah looked at the envelope, torn between ripping into it and tossing it into the trash. Because she had promised Dylan she would contact him immediately if another letter should arrive, she sighed and agreed. "I'll call him. Maybe he should be the one to open it."

It took Dylan less than half an hour to get there. He arrived just after Nathan, whom Deborah had insisted on calling after they'd contacted Dylan. Leaving Nathan in the kitchen with their mother, Deborah hurried to answer when Dylan rang the doorbell.

Dylan took one look at Deborah's face and reached out to place both hands on her shoulders. "Are you okay? You're as pale as a ghost."

It was only because of the trying circumstances that Deborah found such comfort in his concern, she assured herself. And only because she was so tired that his touch made her want to move closer to him. "I'm okay. Just furious that whoever is doing this won't leave us alone."

"Have you read it?"

"No. We thought it best to wait for you and Nathan."

He nodded, his gaze still locked on her face. "Try not to worry too much, Deb. There's no way I would let anything happen to your mother or to anyone else in your family."

"I know that." She struggled for a casual smile. "After all, it is your job."

"It's more than my job, damn it." His voice was rough-edged now, wiping any attempt at a smile from her face. "You know that."

Her eyes locked with his, and what she saw there made her breath lodge in her throat. She couldn't have spoken then even if she had known what to say.

Chapter Eight

It was a great relief to Deborah when Nathan spoke suddenly from behind her, making a reply to Dylan's remark unnecessary.

"Mom's made coffee," Nathan announced. "She said we might as well do this in the kitchen."

Deborah stepped out from beneath Dylan's hands, quickly putting a safe distance between them. She couldn't think about what he might have meant with his comment, she told herself. Nor about how to interpret the look she had seen in his eyes. She had more urgent matters to concentrate on.

She turned and led the way toward the kitchen, knowing that Dylan was close behind her.

Some women, she mused as she moved toward Lenore's kitchen, would have had Dylan escorted to the living room and would have brought the coffee in on a serving tray. Not Lenore. Her kitchen was the place where she was most comfortable, where she reigned supreme. It was the room Lenore retreated to when she was worried or upset, the place where she enjoyed preparing meals and treats for her family.

Unlike her ambitious and career-minded daughter and daughters-in-law, Lenore had never aspired to be more than a wife, a mother and a community volunteer. A comfortable inheritance from her parents and a generous divorce settlement from her successful but philandering husband had ensured that Lenore would never worry about money, but Deborah knew her mother would never quite recover from her disappointment in the way her marriage had ended. Lenore took solace in her family, her friends, her charity—and her kitchen.

"Thank you for coming, Dylan," Lenore said when he entered behind Deborah. "I'm sorry we keep dragging you over here this way."

"No problem, Mrs. McCloud. I hope I can help."

He always spoke to her mother with such respect, Deborah thought. She supposed Lenore was Dylan's ideal of the perfect woman—gracious, genteel, unerringly courteous and infinitely patient. Saintly.

Very much the opposite of Deborah herself.

"Would you like some coffee?" Lenore asked Dylan.

"Yes, thank you."

Lenore could have been hosting a tea party, Deborah thought with a slight shake of her head. The little social niceties were making Deborah impatient, but she knew better than to try to hurry things along. Her mother would only reprimand her for being rude to their guest.

Lenore waved Dylan to a chair. "Please have a seat. The letter is there on the table."

Dylan pulled up a chair, accepted his coffee with a murmur of thanks and waited until everyone else was seated. Only then did he reach for the envelope.

Lenore had served coffee to everyone, but Deborah left hers untouched as she waited tensely for Dylan to scan the single-page letter. "Well? What does it say?"

"Give him time to read it, Deborah," Lenore murmured, sipping her own coffee with a relaxed air that might have fooled anyone who didn't notice her white-knuckled grip on the mug.

Dylan's attention was focused solely on the letter. His gray eyes were narrowed, and his jaw had gone hard. He hissed a curse between his teeth, then looked quickly at Lenore. "Sorry, ma'am."

She gave him a tight smile. "I understand. I've had similar sentiments after reading those letters."

"What does it say?" Deborah asked again.

Rather than read the words aloud, Dylan handed her the sheet of white paper. Nathan scooted his chair closer so he could read over Deborah's shoulder. Both of them were scowling by the time they reached the end of the terse, vitriolic tirade.

Whoever it was who had written the letters was growing increasingly irate at not being taken seriously. There had been no holiday this time, no special family outing. It had been less than a week since the last letter, much closer together than the previous ones. And the threat in this letter was more graphic: Lenore was to stop facilitating Isabelle's integration into Honesty's upper social circles or the entire

McCloud family would pay for their arrogance and presumption.

"Let me see it," Lenore said when it was obvious that Deborah and Nathan had finished.

"You don't want to read this garbage, Mom," Nathan assured her gruffly. "It would just upset you."

"I still want to read it," Lenore insisted, her hand steady as she held it out to them.

Reluctantly, Nathan handed his mother the letter. They watched as she read it, no reaction visible on her face. When she had finished, she looked up, laying the page in front of her. "Yes, you're right," she said evenly. "That is a load of crap."

Dylan was startled into a laugh. Because Deborah and Nathan knew Lenore much better, they weren't particularly surprised by her rare, but characteristic inelegance.

Lenore looked at Dylan. "All right, what do we do now? Ignoring the letters doesn't seem to be working. Should we assume that the sender is disturbed but harmless? Or should we take these threats seriously enough to take steps toward our protection?"

"I think we should take this one as seriously as the previous ones," Dylan replied. "Go about your usual business, but stay on guard. Keep your doors locked and your eyes open. In the meantime, I'll step up my investigation."

"Just what, exactly, does your investigation entail?" Deborah asked, taking her aggravation out on him. "What have you done so far?"

Without any evidence of annoyance at her critical tone, he pulled a small notebook from the pocket of his dark-blue uniform shirt. Flipping it open, he consulted the scribbled notes inside. "I have a list of some of the people who've been the most involved in gossip about your family. Most of the talk is the usual harmless prattle—no more than they say about any of the prominent citizens around here. A few names stood out as being particularly critical of your actions."

Lenore looked at the notebook with distaste. "I'm not sure I want to hear the names. It would be difficult for me to interact politely with people who have been talking disrespectfully about my family."

"Well, *I* want to hear the names," Deborah said, crossing her arms and eyeing the notebook in Dylan's hand. "And I want to know exactly what every one of them said."

Dylan gave her a warning look. "There would be no purpose in me reporting every tidbit of gossip that's gone around since Isabelle arrived. Surely you know that folks in this town—in *any* town—like to talk about everyone else. They've been talking about your family for years, just like they talk about the Sawyers and the Bookers, and my family for that matter."

"And you wonder why I choose to live somewhere else," Deborah said to Nathan.

Nathan shrugged. "There's no gossip in Tampa? Sorry, I don't buy it."

Because she belonged to a health club and a professional women's organization and frequented a fashionable hair styling salon in Tampa, Deborah was well aware that gossip thrived everywhere. But at least in Tampa, they weren't talking about *her* family.

Satisfied that he had made his point, Nathan turned

back to Dylan. "Do any names stand out in your list? Anyone who makes you suspicious?"

"There are a couple I would like to talk to," Dylan answered noncommittally. "Right now, I want to ask each of you to think again about anyone who has acted strangely around you. Anyone who used to be friendly, but has pulled away during the past few months. Anyone who seems uncomfortable around Isabelle."

Deborah shook her head. "Obviously, I don't know anyone. I don't live here. I haven't noticed anyone acting oddly while I've been in town."

Nathan and Lenore looked at each other.

"I've already said I don't have any ideas," Lenore reminded them. "There are a few women in my circles that I don't really care for, but there's no one who has acted any differently than before. Not that I've noticed, anyway."

"I can think of plenty of folks around here who don't like me," Nathan said. "But, hell, I'm a lawyer. We expect that sort of thing."

Dylan smiled briefly. "Then maybe you should make me a list of the people who dislike you most."

Nathan grinned. "I'll have Irene get right on that. If anyone knows who my enemies are, it's my office manager."

"Aren't you going to tell us anyone you might be investigating closely?" Deborah asked Dylan, frustrated that they were making no progress.

Rather than answering her directly, Dylan looked at Lenore. "How's your relationship with your neighbors, Mrs. McCloud?"

"My neighbors?" Lenore seemed surprised by the question.

He nodded. "Any problems there?"

"Not at all. Dr. and Mrs. Cohen live on the north side of my house. Poor Dr. Cohen hasn't been well for the past couple of years—Alzheimer's, I'm afraid. Ruth Ann spends most of her time looking after him. Their son lives in Kansas, but he visits as often as he's able."

"And your other neighbors?"

Deborah looked at Dylan with narrowed eyes, hearing something in his voice that roused her suspicions.

"The Gilberts are across the street. Nice young couple—he does something with computers, and she owns that dress shop on Maple Street. Two teenagers, both well-behaved, though the girl does tend to dress a bit scantily for my idea of propriety."

She took a delicate sip of her coffee before continuing. "I'm sure you know that Lucille Mayo lives on my south side. She's lived there since before Stuart and I bought this house in '73. Her husband passed away five years ago."

"You and Lucille get along?"

"Of course. We grew up together. We were in the same class in school."

"And what has her attitude been toward Isabelle?"

Lenore wrinkled her nose a bit, the expression wry. "Lucille is much too wrapped up in her own grandchildren to be particularly interested in anyone else's. She has five—two boys and three girls. She thinks they're all perfect."

Deborah rubbed her temples, feeling tension and edginess settling there. "You're not in competition with Lucille, Mother. Isabelle is not your grandchild."

"I'm aware of that, Deborah. How do you suggest I refer to her? Step-daughter isn't quite accurate, is it?"

The rather caustic question demonstrated that the pressure was getting to Lenore, as well.

"Mom is making the best of an uncomfortable situation," Nathan reminded his sister with an edge of irritation to his voice. "Caitlin and I want children and we already think of Isabelle as our own. She's only four, damn it. Little more than a baby."

"I know that." Deborah heard the defensiveness in her voice.

Nathan startled them all by slamming his hand on the table, making the cups rattle and coffee splash over the rims. "What kind of vicious, small-minded psycho would spew this sort of venom toward an innocent little girl who never did anything to anyone?"

"Nathan," Lenore reproved, reaching hastily for a napkin. "A tantrum never settled anything."

Nathan drew a deep breath, somewhat calmed by the incongruous reprimand from his youth.

Looking from Nathan to Lenore, Dylan said, "I've been keeping all this pretty quiet because I didn't want to stir up the old gossip again. But I'm going to start looking into it more aggressively now, asking some hard questions, making it clear that this harassment will not be tolerated."

Lenore smiled approvingly at Dylan. "I know you'll take care of this matter for us, Dylan, but do you think you can settle it soon? It's really getting very disturbing."

Deborah watched as one corner of Dylan's firm

mouth tipped upward. "I'll do my best, Mrs. Mc-Cloud."

She nodded as if the matter had been settled. "Would you like some more coffee? A piece of pie, maybe? I have a chocolate pie in the refrigerator."

"No, thank you, ma'am. I have some things to do." He pushed his chair back from the table and rose, the letter in his hand. "I'll take this with me, if you don't mind."

"Of course."

"I'll have some of that chocolate pie, Mom," Nathan said, his expression closer to his usual good humor now. Deborah knew he was making an effort for their mother's sake, but she still saw the embers of smoldering temper in his dark-blue eyes.

"I'll walk you out, Dylan," Deborah said on impulse, jumping to her feet.

He looked a bit surprised, but he nodded farewells to Lenore and Nathan and quietly followed Deborah out of the kitchen.

Deborah led Dylan out the front door, closing it behind them. The sun hadn't set yet, but a spring storm was moving in, darkening the sky with thickening layers of heavy gray clouds. The wind that had blown the clouds their way caught at Deborah's hair, blowing several strands into her face. She reached up to tuck them behind her ear as she turned to Dylan on the front porch.

"Why did you seem particularly interested in Lucille Mayo?" she asked. "Surely you don't think she's the one sending the letters."

"I didn't say that."

"Then why the questions? And why did I get the feeling there was something you weren't telling us?"

He shrugged, glancing toward the brick-and-white-siding house next door. "I'll admit it seems unlikely that Mrs. Mayo would be behind this. She was my ninth-grade English teacher."

"Mine, too. She's still teaching, actually, though I've heard she's retiring at the end of this school year."

"It's just that she's one of the town's more active gossips. While I haven't heard anything she has said that was particularly hostile toward Isabelle, or anyone else in your immediate family, she has talked quite a bit about the situation."

Deborah turned to glare toward Lucille's house, her fists clenched on her hips. A rumble of thunder in the distance seemed to put voice to her bad mood. "Maybe Lucille would like to talk to *me*."

Dylan rested a hand on her shoulder. "Just let me handle this, okay? I'll find a way to talk to Lucille without causing hard feelings between her and your mother."

"I don't know why Mother would care to remain on good terms with someone who talks about our family behind our backs."

Dylan applied enough pressure on her shoulder to turn her around to face him. The outside lights hadn't come on yet, so they stood in purply shadows within the deep porch. Deborah had no trouble seeing Dylan's face. Though he wasn't smiling, there was a note of humor in his voice when he asked, "Are you telling me your mother never indulges in any gossip with the other ladies in her community groups?"

Deborah opened her mouth to assure him of just that, but she closed it again before she could say something she knew would be untrue.

"I'm sure Mother indulges in occasional gossip," she admitted reluctantly. "But she is never malicious. Especially after what our family went through five years ago, we know how much harm idle talk can do."

"I didn't say your mother was ever malicious," he reminded her. "And I told you I haven't heard that Lucille has been, either. I just think she's plugged into the grapevine firmly enough to be a potential source of information for us."

Deborah sighed and let some of her angry tension ebb, her shoulders relaxing a bit beneath his hands. "You're right. I guess I'm primed for a fight against whoever is harassing my mother."

"I don't blame you. I feel very much the same way."

She nodded slowly. "I'm just not accustomed to standing back and letting other people fight my battles for me."

He flashed one of his rare, full smiles. "Is that right? I never would have guessed that about you."

Humor had drawn them together all those years ago. Deborah couldn't resist returning his smile, though hers felt strained. "Okay, I'll back off. Or at least I'll try," she amended. "I have to admit I'm impatient to have this settled before I go back to Tampa next week."

She felt what might have been a slight spasm tighten his fingers on her shoulders. And then he released her and took a step backward, his arms falling to his side, all hint of a smile leaving his face.

"Speaking of gossip," he said, "I've heard rumors you might be moving back to Honesty if Lindsey Newman has her way."

Deborah frowned. "She told you?"

Had Dylan called Lindsey since lunch Wednesday? Had he taken Lindsey's blatant hints and asked her out? A heavy sensation settled in Deborah's stomach in response to that possibility, a feeling she tried hard to ignore. After all, she told herself, it was absolutely none of her business.

"No, I haven't spoken to Lindsey since I left the two of you at the restaurant Wednesday."

The heavy feeling immediately lightened. And then settled again because she was annoyed with herself for caring who Dylan dated. Scowling, more at herself than at him, she asked, "Then who told you?"

His mouth twisted. "Let's just say I heard it through the grapevine."

"Oh. Well—" Wrapping her arms around herself as if to ward off a chill from the rain-promising wind, she looked toward the west, where flashes of distant lightning danced across the clouds. "As I suppose someone has told you, Lindsey plans to invest in an office-furniture franchise, and she has offered me a partnership because of my design experience."

"How's her business plan? Sound?"

"Yes, she has certainly done the research. I think she can make a go of it."

He was also watching the skies now, and he spoke almost off-handedly, but Deborah sensed that he was deeply interested when he asked, "You thinking about taking her up on it?"

"It's intriguing, I'll admit, but I don't think so."

Dylan turned back to face her then. "Why not?"

"Several reasons."

"Am I one of them?"

She swallowed. "Why would you have anything to do with my career plans?"

"Maybe you don't want to move back to Honesty because I live here."

She attempted a derisive chuckle. "Giving yourself a lot of credit, aren't you? Believe it or not, I don't base any of my decisions on you. You're just not that important to me."

Because she had been avoiding looking at him, she didn't realize he had moved until he spoke in her ear. When had he learned to move so silently?

"I was important to you once," he murmured.

Another flash of lightning skittered across the horizon, followed several seconds later by a low rumble of thunder. It took Deborah a beat longer than that before she trusted herself to speak without emotion. "Yes, you were important to me once. Too important, actually. I was so wrapped up in you that I could hardly think for myself. Girlhood infatuations can be so overwhelming."

"Girlhood infatuations?" It was obvious that he disapproved of her choice of words.

She shrugged. "Of course. But I was a different person then. I've grown up since."

Heartbreak and disillusionment had a way of bringing childhood to an end. Dylan and her father had both contributed to the demise of her own.

"I've done a lot of growing up myself," he said, reaching out to brush a wind-tossed strand of hair away from her eyes. "I would do a lot of things differently, now."

If he was implying that he would like another chance with her, she needed to set him straight immediately and emphatically. No way would she allow herself to be drawn back into another overwhelming and all-consuming relationship with Dylan. No matter what he said about things being different now, she remembered the pain she had suffered last time all too clearly.

As had become her pattern during the past seven years, she reacted to the bad memories by pushing them very firmly to the back of her mind and putting a heavy mental lid on them. If she didn't acknowledge them, they couldn't hurt her. That philosophy had served her well enough. She saw no reason to change it now.

"Didn't we agree not to talk about the past?" she said, turning partially away from him. "All I'm interested in now is finding out who is bothering my mother with those creepy letters."

He studied her face through narrowed eyes. "You seem to be afraid to discuss the past with me. Maybe you aren't completely over those old feelings, after all?"

"Don't be ridiculous. I am completely over that infatuation."

"So my touch no longer affects you the way it once did?" He ran his fingertips slowly along the line of her jaw and across her lower lip, a gesture that had never failed to make her tremble.

She told herself she shivered now only because of the slight chill in the damp early-evening air.

It was a presumptuous move quite characteristic of the Dylan she remembered. The reckless, impulsive, hot-headed young man who had swooped into her life and made her fall totally, completely, almost insanely in love with him, so blindly besotted that she had been willing to sacrifice everything for him.

She had eagerly left behind her virginity and her old crowd of teenage friends for him. She had been prepared to abandon her plans for the future. And she had almost been willing to estrange herself from her disapproving family. Almost. It had been her reluctance to make that final break that had been the last straw between her and Dylan.

The breakup had been ugly. Cutting. Angry.

Deborah was the only one who knew that night had almost ended tragically. Or that she had just barely survived it.

It hurt too much to remember that night or the weeks and months that had followed. She shook her head as if to clear her mind of the memories.

"Stop it, Dylan," she said crossly. "This isn't—"

"I'm merely questioning your point that you have no feelings left for me," he said, his fingers stroking her throat now. "I suppose you wouldn't respond even if I were to, say, kiss you?"

"No, I wouldn't," she snapped, losing patience with whatever game he was playing. "Now, would you just—"

"Prove it," he said, just before his mouth settled over hers.

As familiar as his kisses had once been, there was something different about this one. Something more than the passage of time. More than the feel of a metal badge pressing against her right breast or the weapon and other police paraphernalia he wore at his waist. Dylan had changed. As had she.

But the chemistry between them was still powerful.

Her temporary paralysis ending, she pushed against him, breaking the contact between them. Her lips felt damp and tender from his kiss, but she kept them from trembling by forming them into a fierce frown.

"I hate you for that," she said.

Proving that she could never predict how Dylan was going to react to anything, he laughed. "No, you don't," he said, running a hand over her hair in a gesture that was almost indulgent. "But we'll leave it at that for tonight."

He turned then and walked to his car, his steps a rolling cowboy amble. If there was any justice in the world, the incipient lightning would strike right at his feet, Deborah thought, glaring after him. She didn't want to seriously injure him, just to make the world rock around him a little.

It would be only fair, considering what he had just done to her.

Chapter Nine

Much to Lenore's anticipation, Gideon and Adrienne were due home from their honeymoon Saturday afternoon. They'd taken only a week away, but Deborah thought Adrienne was lucky to have had that long. Gideon wasn't much of a traveler, preferring to spend his time locked in the office of his secluded country cottage where he created the paranormal thrillers that were rapidly turning him into a very successful author.

Deborah wondered if the book Dylan had written was anything like those that Gideon wrote. And whether Dylan would quit his job with the police department when his book was published. Maybe he would even move away from Honesty to seek out the glamorous celebrity lifestyle that Gideon so assiduously avoided.

"I'll make my spinach lasagna for dinner this evening," Lenore said during breakfast as she happily anticipated being surrounded by her family that evening. "With a big salad and some crusty rolls and a couple of different desserts to follow. How does that sound?"

"Sounds great, Mother," Deborah replied around a big yawn.

Lenore looked at her sympathetically. "Did the storm keep you awake last night?"

"Um, sure. That was what kept me awake," Deborah said a bit too quickly.

It was much more comfortable for her to attribute her sleepless night to the noisy fury of a spring storm than to the lingering effects of a brief, uninvited kiss.

"It was quite a storm, wasn't it? I'm just glad no damage was done."

"Yes, so am I." No damage was done at all, Deborah assured herself. Dylan had kissed her and she had survived the experience without falling under his spell again. All it had cost her was a few hours sleep.

"I think I'll invite Aunt Betty for dinner," Lenore mused aloud.

Deborah choked on a bite of bagel. "Why would you want to do that?"

Lenore fingered the pearls at her throat. "We haven't had her join us in a while."

"There's a reason for that." Deborah's paternal great-aunt was six feet tall, weighed more than two hundred pounds and had a voice loud enough to rattle all the windows in the house. Last night's storm had nothing on Betty in either volume or potential for leaving chaos in her wake.

"We have to be gracious, Deborah. Aunt Betty is family."

Lenore's generous interpretation of the word, Deborah reflected. Betty had been married to Stuart's late uncle—a kinship that was distant, to say the least. And yet Lenore still felt obliged to include the older woman in family events at regular intervals.

"It's your party, Mother. Invite whoever you want."

Lenore made a notation on the pad she always kept in her efficiently organized kitchen. "I believe I'll call Lindsey Newman, too. You and she seem to have renewed your friendship this week, and she and Caitlin have been friends for some time. Maybe she would enjoy having dinner with the family."

Deborah shifted uncomfortably in her seat. She hadn't mentioned Lindsey's business proposition to her mother yet, and now she wondered if that had been a mistake. But Lenore had been dealing with her own concerns. Deborah hadn't wanted to give Lenore more to worry about, nor had she wanted to give her mother false hopes that Deborah had plans to move back to Honesty.

"Lindsey may well have something else to do on a Saturday evening," she said.

"Very likely," Lenore agreed. "But I think I'll give her a call, anyway."

"I need to tell you something first." Deborah drew a deep breath and then launched into a concise explanation of why she had been meeting with Lindsey during the past few days.

Lenore didn't look particularly surprised. "I figured it must be something like that."

"Why? What have you heard?"

"Not much, really. I just knew there must be a reason you and Lindsey were meeting. I assumed you would tell me when you were ready. Have you made any decisions?''

The question was asked casually, Lenore being very careful not to imply any opinion of her own, yet Deborah knew her answer was important to her mother.

''No, I haven't made a decision. There are a lot of things to consider. I'm not sure I'm ready to go into business on my own, even with a partner. As much as I like Lindsey, I don't know how well we would work together on a long-term basis. I worry about the odds against any new business making it past the first two years. And finally, but very importantly, I'm not at all sure I want to move back to Honesty.''

''Because of Dylan,'' Lenore murmured as though it were more fact than supposition.

Deborah let out an explosive sigh. ''No, not because of Dylan. Honestly, Mother.''

''Well, I can't think of any other reason why you would be so reluctant to move here. Honesty is a lovely place to live. Low crime, clean air, a strengthening economic base. And your family is here.''

''So are the most active gossips in the state of Mississippi,'' Deborah retorted. ''Maybe I like living where no one knows every detail of my personal business. Where my older brothers aren't nearby to boss me around.''

''And away from your mother and the little sister you're still having so much trouble acknowledging?''

The quiet question brought Deborah's chin up. ''It has nothing to do with you, either. You know I would enjoy seeing you more.''

''And Isabelle?''

Deborah sat back in her chair. ''Isabelle is Nathan's responsibility. I have nothing against her, and I'm glad she has brought you so much pleasure. I'm furious that someone has made veiled threats against my family because of her, but I certainly don't blame Isabelle for anything.''

''But you still have trouble accepting her as your sister.''

Deborah abruptly changed the subject. ''What do you need me to do to help with your dinner party?''

Lenore sighed, but went along cooperatively enough. ''You could run to the grocery store for me. I have a list of a few things I need.''

''I would be happy to,'' Deborah agreed almost too eagerly. At least this would give her a chance to get away from her mother's worried looks for a little while.

Half an hour later she walked out the front door, the grocery list tucked into the pocket of her low-slung flared jeans. A bright-yellow short-sleeve pull-over was sufficient for the humid warmth the thunderstorm had left in its wake. Small puddles of rainwater on the walkway squished beneath the soles of her gray-and-yellow running shoes as she moved to her car, which she had left parked in the driveway rather than in her mother's garage.

She frowned as she approached the silver-blue sports car, the remote entry controller in her hand. Something about her car looked odd, as if it were sitting at a funny angle.

''Son of a—'' She skidded to a halt, staring in disbelief at her deflated tires.

Fury slammed through her, causing her to throw her crocheted bag to the ground and kick one of the flattened tires. A string of colorful curses escaped her, accompanied by another couple of kicks.

"Deborah?" Standing on her front lawn, apparently retrieving her morning newspaper, Lucille Mayo called to her. "Are you all right?"

Still steaming, Deborah took a few steps toward the neighboring house. "Someone slashed my tires."

The older woman looked genuinely shocked. "Slashed your tires? You mean vandalism?"

"You could say that. Have you seen anyone over here since last night?"

"Why, no, I haven't seen anyone since your brother and Officer Smith left here last night."

Of course Lucille had seen their visitors, Deborah thought. With Deborah's luck, Lucille had probably seen a certain ill-advised kiss, as well—and would spread the news about that all over town. So why hadn't the nosy neighbor seen anything useful last night?

"I went to bed rather early," Lucille said, as if feeling the need to explain her oversight. "And then there was that terrible storm…"

Deborah reined in her temper enough to speak cordially. "You'd better make sure there's been no damage at your place. Sometimes vandals hit more than one house on a street."

But even as Lucille scurried away to check her own valuables, Deborah knew the search would be fruitless. This wasn't a random act of vandalism. This was a very personal message.

Dylan wasn't usually a late sleeper, even on weekends when he didn't have to work, but he hadn't slept very well Friday night. There had been the achy restlessness left over from that all-too-brief kiss, for one thing.

Then had come the storm, the wind and rain hammering against the roof of his mobile home. The dogs had started howling, and Dylan had spent most of the night pacing, making sure everything was secure. He'd considered doing some writing, trying to accomplish something worthwhile during the long dark hours, but the electricity kept flickering and his laptop battery was down. Since his handwriting was generally illegible even to himself, he didn't like to write with pen and paper.

So, he had stood at the glass doors for hours looking out toward the lake, and every time he'd seen the lightning reflected in the water, he had remembered the way Deborah had looked as she watched the storm approaching from her mother's front porch. Just before he had kissed her.

He knew she would make him pay for that, but he didn't regret it. The kiss had answered a couple of questions for him. Deborah might not have forgiven him for the past, but she hadn't forgotten it. And she might say she hated him—maybe she did in some ways—but the attraction was still strong between them. And it wasn't only on his part.

When he had finally tumbled into bed as the storm abated, he'd had to force himself to put thoughts of Deborah completely out of his mind before he could sleep. It was a pounding on his front door that woke him hours later.

Groggy and disoriented, he peered at the clock, surprised to find that it was almost eleven. He hadn't slept this late in years, not since he'd stopped staying out late drinking with his buddies.

Rolling out of the rumpled bed, he stepped into the jeans he'd left lying on the floor. Tugging at the zipper, he left the snap unfastened as he walked barefoot through the trailer to the front door.

Identifying Deborah through the door window, he pushed a hand through his short hair as he reached for the doorknob.

She looked taken aback by his appearance. "You were in bed?"

"Yeah."

Glancing past him, she cleared her throat. "Um—"

"Yes, alone," he answered her unspoken question, his tone curt. Turning abruptly away from the door, he snapped, "I need coffee."

He heard her scramble after him, closing the door behind her. "Dylan—"

"Coffee first." He reached for the carafe of the automatic coffeemaker, relieved that he had remembered to set the timer before he'd turned in. He assumed Deborah was here to chew him out for kissing her last night and probably to remind him that cows would rule the world before she would ever consider getting involved with him again. He needed caffeine before he could deal with that lecture. "Want some?"

"No, thanks. I had breakfast hours ago."

A dig about how late he had slept. He let it pass, having no desire to tell her just what had kept him up so late.

Taking a bracing sip of his coffee, he turned to lean against the counter behind him. He studied Deborah's face over the rim of his mug, noting that she seemed to be having trouble looking at him. Maybe he should have put on a shirt.

"Okay, I'm somewhat coherent now," he said. "Why are you here?"

"Someone slashed my tires last night."

"Damn it!" He hastily set his mug down, then wiped off the scalding coffee that had splashed onto his hand when he'd jerked. "Why the hell didn't you tell me this before?"

"You wouldn't let me speak." She planted her fists on her hips, finally meeting his eyes. "Why did you think I was here? A social call?"

"Never mind what I thought. Tell me exactly what happened."

She shrugged, her voice resentful. "Sometime between when I went to bed around midnight and when I went out to my car at about nine-thirty, someone repeatedly stuck a knife or a screwdriver or something sharp into all the tires on my car. They're ruined. Lucille Mayo said she didn't see anything, and the other neighbors said the same thing when Mother called them. No one else had any damage done to their property."

"I don't think this was a roving band of juvenile delinquents."

"Neither do I." She crossed her arms. "It's a message to us. I'm afraid it's a first strike."

"Did you call the station?"

"Yes. Officer Buckwalter came to fill out a report. He said you were off duty today."

She was scared, he realized, or she wouldn't have come to him. And he couldn't blame her. This was more than an anonymous letter. This was a destructive attack and it had happened only yards from where she and her mother had slept.

It was enough to shake *him,* too.

"I'm sure Pat's doing what he can to find leads," he assured her. "But if none of the neighbors saw anything unusual, it's unlikely he'll make an arrest."

"Just when are you people going to do something about this?" Deborah demanded, her eyes going almost navy with emotion. "In only a little less than a week, we've received two threatening letters and I've had my tires slashed. Are you going to wait until someone physically attacks one of us before you put a stop to it?"

"We're doing the best we can, Deb. I'm taking several days off patrol just to talk to as many people as I can to track down any leads. I'll start today, as soon as I've showered and dressed. I'm not on duty today, so I can spend all afternoon on it."

"And while you're talking to every chatterbox in town, what are we supposed to do? Sit around and wait for the next attack? Trust that no one is going to go through with their threats to make my mother pay for being generous and kind-hearted?"

He could sense anxiety mounting in her as she fought for control. He knew Deborah well enough to understand that, as tough as she tried to act, any threat to her mother was enough to terrify her.

He placed his hands on her shoulders and looked directly into her eyes. "Deborah. We're not going to let anything happen to your mother. There will be extra patrols around her house and everyone will be notified to keep an eye out for her."

"I hate this," she told him fiercely.

"I know. So do I. I'm the only one who's supposed to be giving you headaches."

It was a deliberate attempt to calm her down, and it seemed to work. She even smiled a little. "You are very good at that."

"I'm glad to know you think I'm good at something."

A hint of color tinted her too-pale cheeks. "I suppose I'd better let you get to work," she said, lowering her eyes from his face. And then her gaze skittered away from his bare chest, as if seeing it made her uncomfortable.

"Just a minute." He was reluctant to let her step away. She felt so good beneath his hands.

The top of her blond head came just to his eye level, and she stood close enough that her breasts almost brushed his chest when she inhaled. The aching that had plagued him all night returned full force, settling low in his groin. His fingers tightened spasmodically on her shoulders, crumpling the yellow knit fabric of her shirt. "Deb—"

The look she gave him then held a mixture of warning and wariness. "Don't."

"I've spent most of my adult life trying not to want you," he said gruffly, his gaze on her trembling mouth. "I still haven't figured out how to make it work."

"I am not going to do this," she said, and her expression was as ardent as her voice. "I'm not setting myself up for disaster again."

"I agree." He moved his hands on her shoulders, feeling the tension knotted in her muscles. "It would be a big mistake for us to get involved again the way we were before."

Though she seemed suspicious of his apparent turn-around, she nodded. "Absolutely."

His thumbs rotated at the base of her neck, causing her to flex involuntarily in response. "After all, you're only in town for another few days. And both of us have many more things to think about right now."

"True." Her eyelids fluttered a bit as she relaxed gradually into his gentle kneading.

"The fact that we're still strongly attracted to each other on a physical level is completely irrelevant."

"Exactly." Her eyelids suddenly lifted as his words—and her agreement—sank in. "I mean—"

She hadn't denied it, he thought in satisfaction. It was a small step, but he was willing to take what he could get at this point.

"Then we're agreed. We can work together to help your mother without resurrecting the past."

She nodded somewhat uncertainly. "That would be best."

It was the first time in years she had agreed with him on much of anything. Now would be a good time for him to release her and step away, before he did something stupid and ticked her off again.

He didn't want to resurrect the stormy, immature, almost too-consuming connection they'd had before. But he wanted very much to start something new with her. And this time make it work.

Pushing too hard now was no way to begin.

Ordering himself to let her go and step away, he loosened his fingers. And then he made the mistake of looking into her eyes.

Tension radiated through them both, holding them frozen in place. Dylan felt his breath lodge hard in his throat as past emotions mingled with present desires, urging him to pull her closer.

Probably to ward him off, she laid her hands on his bare chest. His muscles contracted beneath her cool touch, accompanied by the hiss of his sharply indrawn breath.

"Don't," she whispered, her blue eyes so dark now they looked almost black.

It wasn't easy for him to speak through the pulse pounding in his throat, but he managed to say, "I won't do anything you don't want."

Her fingers spread a little against him, as if to feel more of him. He wasn't sure if the movement was intentional or involuntary, but it had a powerful effect on him.

Deborah lowered her gaze to her hands, studying them against his tanned, lightly furred chest. "I'm not sure I was talking to you," she murmured, slowly moving her hands again.

So it had been herself she'd been warning. Proving yet again that the temptation was not all one-sided.

Her eyes lifted very slowly to his again. "I've spent the past seven years hating you. I'm comfortable with that. I'm not sure I want to change it."

Suddenly annoyed, he drew her closer. "Since you're determined to hate me, anyway..."

He noticed that she didn't resist as he closed his mouth over hers.

Deborah hadn't been thinking very clearly since Dylan had opened his door to her, having very obviously just been roused from his bed. His coffee-colored hair had been rumpled into spikes, his gray eyes were sleepy-lidded, and his hard jaw was stubbled with dark shadow. He had looked grouchy and sexy and more than a little dangerous.

On top of that, he'd been half-naked, wearing nothing but a pair of jeans. He was no longer the skinny boy she remembered. His shoulders seemed wider now, his arms and torso more solid and muscular. A smattering of fine dark hairs covered his chest and arrowed down to his intriguingly unfastened jeans.

She had taken one look at him and nearly lost her capacity for speech. It had actually been a relief that he'd wanted to drink some coffee before talking; it had given her a chance to get her scattered thoughts together.

And then he had touched her. Gazed into her eyes. And told her that he still wanted her. Damn him.

His lips were hard against hers, his beard rough against her face. He'd implied that he kissed her out of irritation. Payback, in a way, for her assertion that she hated him and that she wasn't interested in rectifying that situation.

But the kiss didn't feel like a rebuke. If she hadn't known better, she would have sworn she was being rewarded for something very special.

No one had ever kissed her like Dylan. It was more than a joining of lips, almost as though they connected on a cellular and molecular level. As if he tasted her soul, and she his.

Not that she had kissed many men. The specter of her relationship with Dylan had hovered over every date she had attempted since. It had rarely seemed worth the effort.

She wondered how many women Dylan had kissed on his self-admitted quest to forget her.

The thought made her draw back a few inches,

breaking the kiss. She didn't remember sliding her arms around Dylan's neck, but there they were.

She moistened her lips, tasting him on them. "Dylan—"

A low groan escaped him. "You don't hate me nearly enough yet," he muttered and kissed her again.

This time he pulled her closer, wrapping his strong arms around her, deepening the kiss until she was lost in it. And even as it thrilled her, it broke her heart, because she knew that she still hadn't banished the ghosts that had haunted her since they had separated.

Maybe she never would.

"Don't, Deb." He sounded as shaken as she felt. His unsteady fingertips moved over her cheeks, smearing the tears she hadn't realized she was shedding.

She *never* cried. Ever. She hadn't allowed herself to do so since she had sobbed her heart out seven years ago. She hadn't cried when her father shattered the family's foundation. She hadn't even cried when he had died almost four years later.

She would be damned if she would cry now in front of Dylan.

Angrily dashing at her cheeks, she spun away from him. It had been a mistake getting that close—one she wouldn't make again.

"Find the person who's annoying my mother," she ordered him coldly. "That's all I want from you."

"Deb, I'm sorry…"

She couldn't look at him as she moved swiftly toward the door. ''I have to go.''

She heard a low curse from behind her, but Dylan didn't try to stop her as she made her escape.

Chapter Ten

Deborah was not in the mood for a party.

Lenore's living room was filled with people Saturday evening. Every available seat was taken, and the noise level was high, mostly due to the oversize matron who held court in the most comfortable chair, her booming voice drowning out any other attempt at conversation.

Newlyweds Gideon and Adrienne sat on the couch, Isabelle perched on Gideon's knee. Thirty-one-year-old Gideon was the dark-haired, green-eyed changeling among Stuart McCloud's blue-eyed, golden-haired offspring. Dark-eyed, auburn-haired Adrienne looked like the sleek New York literary agent she was, but with a warmth that immediately put other people at ease.

It always took Deborah aback to see Gideon with Isabelle. Gideon had never been interested in children and had made it clear that if Nathan took Isabelle in, Gideon wanted nothing to do with the child.

His attitude had changed in March when a series of circumstances had resulted in Gideon being responsible for Isabelle at the same time his agent had arrived in town to discuss business with him. Because Gideon had been overdue on a deadline, Adrienne had agreed to stay for a few days to help him out with the child. By the end of a week, Gideon had fallen hard for both Adrienne and Isabelle, to the amazement of his family.

Not far from Gideon and Adrienne, Nathan and Caitlin shared a loveseat. Closest to Aunt Betty's chair, they were making a valiant effort to carry on a conversation with the older woman. On the other side of the room, Lindsey Newman sat with Lenore in matching wingback chairs, engaged in an animated discussion that made Deborah a bit uneasy. She would bet they were talking about her.

Deborah moved around the room, too restless to sit, and too distracted to join a conversation. Instead, she listened to snippets of what the others were saying as she drifted among them.

Isabelle was babbling to Gideon and Adrienne about everything that had happened at preschool during the week they had been away. "…and then Danny—you remember Danny? The one who said mean things about my daddy? He broke Tiffany's Power Puff Girls pencil box, and Tiffany got so mad! She said she's never going to talk to Danny again, and Ms. Montgomery…"

Having little interest in preschool politics, Deborah moved on.

Aunt Betty was berating Nathan for representing a

man she knew in an ugly divorce. "You're trying to help him leave poor Georgia penniless."

Always the most patient of the McCloud siblings, Nathan managed to respond politely, "Of course I'm not at liberty to talk about my client's business, but Georgia won't be left penniless, Aunt Betty. I'm simply making sure there's a fair settlement for everyone involved."

"What's fair about a sixty-five-year-old man leaving his wife of forty years because he claims he wants to spend the rest of his days fishing in peace? Most irresponsible thing I ever heard. You didn't see my Mitch divorcing me because I wouldn't let him spend every waking hour on the golf course, which he would have done if I hadn't reminded him frequently that there were more important things to do."

No, Deborah thought on her way past, poor old Uncle Mitch had just quietly died, instead. He'd had a heart attack on a golf course. The three friends golfing with him on that beautiful spring afternoon had sworn he was smiling when he slipped away.

Lenore looked up from her conversation with Lindsey. "For heaven's sake, Deborah, will you light somewhere? You're making me nervous pacing around like a cat."

Deborah sighed. "I'm getting sort of hungry. Is there something I can do in the kitchen to help with dinner?"

She wasn't at all hungry, actually, but she couldn't spend much more time in this room, pretending that nothing was bothering her, when exactly the opposite was true. She was worried about the letters and the slashed tires. She still hadn't made a definitive decision about Lindsey's business proposition.

And then there was Dylan....

"Surely there's something I can do in the kitchen," she said quickly, needing to do something—*anything*—to keep her mind and hands busy.

Lenore stood. "Come along. We'll get dinner on the table."

"Is there anything I can do to help, Mrs. Mc-Cloud?" Lindsey asked.

"No, thank you, dear. Everything's almost ready. Why don't you chat with Caitlin for a few minutes? She looks as though she needs rescuing."

Lindsey glanced at Caitlin, whose smile was beginning to look very strained. "I'll do my best."

"What is it with you this evening, Deborah?" Lenore asked as soon as she and her daughter were alone in the kitchen. "You act as if you're expecting someone to burst through the front door at any moment."

"I know." Deborah tucked a lock of hair behind her left ear in a nervous gesture. "This whole thing is freaking me out."

"It's upsetting all of us, dear. But we cannot let this small-minded person interfere any more than necessary with our routines. We have our family all together this evening, and we should be able to enjoy each other. You're certainly not the type to let someone else run your life."

"I know," Deborah said again. "I'm just having trouble putting it aside."

"Here, you can slice these tomatoes." Having assigned Deborah a task, Lenore turned back to her other last-minute dinner preparations. "You've been especially jumpy since you returned from Dylan's house. Did he say something to disturb you?"

"No." It wasn't what he had said that had disturbed her. It was what he had done. Rocked her world. Destroyed her illusions that she was completely in control of her reaction to him.

"I'm sure he'll take care of this little problem for us," Lenore said confidently. "He seems quite determined to do so."

Little problem. Deborah shook her head as she sliced through a fat tomato. That was one way to refer to it, she supposed. "Yes, he's even spending his day off tracking down rumors."

"That's very thoughtful of him, especially considering his history with our family. I'm glad you and he have settled your differences and that he's made at least a tentative peace with Gideon. It's always so much nicer to be friendly with one's neighbors, don't you think?"

Deborah started to tell Lenore that she and Dylan hadn't even begun to settle any differences. Since that comment might lead to a discussion she didn't want to get into, she merely nodded, instead.

"Dylan's Aunt Myra called me this afternoon. She said she'd heard we were having problems, and she wanted to offer her sympathy and see if there's anything she can do to help us. It was very thoughtful of her to call."

"Yes, it was." Deborah had always gotten along well with Dylan's aunt and uncle while she and Dylan were dating, though she had seen little of them since the breakup.

She and Dylan hadn't spent much time with either of their families when they were dating. Deborah's father had been vehemently against the match, repeatedly stating his belief that Dylan was trouble, and that Deborah could do better. Her overprotective brothers had agreed, especially Gideon, who'd had an adversarial relationship with Dylan dating back to a school hallway skirmish. Obviously, Dylan hadn't felt welcome at Deborah's home.

Actually, they had been so wrapped up in each other that they hadn't felt the need to spend time with anyone else. It had worried Deborah's family that she had cut off ties with all her old friends to spend all her free time with Dylan.

"Myra specifically asked about you," Lenore added very casually. "She said she was sorry your car was targeted so hatefully, and she asked how you were holding up. I told her that you had borrowed my car to go discuss the situation with Dylan. She seemed pleased that you trusted Dylan's competence to help us."

"I have never questioned Dylan's competence." From the time she had first met him, Deborah had believed Dylan could do anything he set his mind to. She had believed in him long before he had believed in himself.

Of course, back then he hadn't expressed interest in being a police officer or a writer. He had worked in construction and had talked vaguely about maybe owning his own contracting business someday. She supposed his uncle had led him into law enforcement. She didn't know where the writing urge had come from.

"The tomatoes are sliced," she said, more than ready to change the subject. "Now what?"

A few minutes later, the meal was on the table. Moving to the living room to call the others to dinner,

Deborah found Lindsey in the process of entertaining the family with a funny story.

"So then Kirk Sawyer," she was saying as Deborah entered the room, "who was trying to be all cool and everything, took a step backward and fell into the fountain. He was drunk, of course. He just sat there with water coming out of the fish's mouth and pouring right onto Kirk's head."

Everyone laughed except Isabelle, who was playing with a couple of dolls on the floor beside the couch, and Betty, who pursed her lips and shook her gray head. "That Sawyer boy has gotten out of control. Driving around in that red sports car like a bat out of hell, putting decent, law-abiding citizens in fear for their lives. You shouldn't have gotten him out of trouble so many times, Nathan. It would have done him a world of good to pay the consequences for some of his actions."

"I don't represent Kirk anymore, Aunt Betty."

"But you did, for entirely too long. I know your daddy pushed you into this career, but it's a shame you couldn't have gotten into something more respectable. I don't know what *you* were thinking, Caitlin. Did your parents pressure you into law school, too?"

Deborah could almost see Caitlin clinging to her patience. "No, my parents always encouraged me to do anything I wanted. I chose law school because it interested me."

"Pity."

Deborah judged that to be a good time to intercede.

"Dinner's ready," she announced loudly, then stepped to one side to allow the others to precede her into the dining room. She wasn't looking forward to sitting at a table for the next hour or so with her outspoken great-aunt.

Gideon hung back with Deborah after the others left the room. "You okay?"

She nodded. "Just antsy."

"Betty can make anyone antsy," Gideon muttered with a glance toward the dining room that proved he was no more looking forward to the meal than Deborah was.

"True."

"Not to mention the jerk who slashed your tires." As much as Lenore had hated spoiling Gideon's homecoming from his honeymoon, she and Deborah had agreed that Gideon needed to be informed about what had been going on in his absence.

Deborah wouldn't have been entirely surprised if Gideon had received a few letters, himself. But apparently whoever had sent them had known writing Gideon would be a waste of time, since he would be neither intimidated nor influenced by anonymous letters. Gideon didn't even open his mail all that often.

As Deborah had expected, Gideon had been coldly infuriated by the report his mother had given him. He'd wanted to find someone immediately and exact revenge, and he had been extremely frustrated that they couldn't give him a name. Hearing that his old enemy was on the case did not visibly reassure him.

"What the hell has Smith been doing?" he had demanded. "Twiddling his thumbs?"

Lenore had assured him that Dylan was doing all he could. Her tone had made it clear that she hadn't wanted to hear any more criticism of Dylan's efforts on her behalf.

But as they lingered in the living room behind

everyone else, Deborah could tell that Gideon wasn't willing to completely trust Dylan to handle the situation. "I think we should consider hiring some protection for Mother until this is resolved," he said. "Maybe for Isabelle, too."

"Bodyguards?" Deborah lifted her eyebrows. "You don't think Mother will agree to that, do you? Especially for herself."

"I'm not sure we should give her the option to refuse. This person is crazy, Deborah. Slashing your tires shows just how reckless they're getting."

"What bothers me is that I've planned to go back to Tampa Thursday. I need to get back, but I hate to leave with this unsettled."

"Nathan and I will keep an eye out for Mom."

"I know. But you also know how hard it is to keep up with her. She's out running around nearly all day every day with all her clubs and activities. How can you keep an eye on her and still have a life of your own?"

"That's why I suggested a bodyguard. At the very least I'll want a detailed daily itinerary from her."

"She isn't going to like that, either." And Deborah couldn't blame her. She would hate to think anyone, even her family, was keeping that close an eye on *her*.

"Tough," Gideon said succinctly. "And what's with you running to Dylan Smith for help, anyway? I thought you hated the guy."

She shrugged. "I hate the guy," she agreed casually. "I'm reserving judgment on the cop."

"You're not going to let him charm you again, are you?" Gideon asked suspiciously. "He's already got Adrienne practically eating out of his hand."

His disgruntled tone made her smile. "You know Adrienne is crazy about you."

"I didn't say I was jealous of him. I'm just not overly pleased that they've become such good buddies."

"I understand she signed him as a client. You want to tell me how *that* happened?"

Scowling, Gideon started to answer, but was sidetracked when Lenore appeared in the doorway. "Aren't you two coming? We're waiting for you."

Sighing in unison, Gideon and Deborah obediently followed their mother to the dining room.

Deborah was beginning to wonder if she would ever sleep again. Every time she closed her eyes she saw Dylan the way he had appeared at his door that morning, all rumpled and grumpy and so damned sexy that it had almost physically hurt to look at him.

Had she seen him looking that way seven years ago, she would have melted into a puddle at his feet. It had been a close enough call this time.

And when he had kissed her…

She muttered a curse and rolled over to punch her pillow. This was an image she did not want in her head.

So instead she lay there thinking about how his bare skin had felt beneath her palms. With a loud groan, she shoved herself out of the bed and began to pace.

Her restless prowling took her to the window. For lack of anything better to do, she moved the curtain aside and looked out. The curse that escaped her then had nothing to do with her uncomfortable memories.

* * *

Dylan sat in his car—the classic dark-green TransAm, not the cruiser—and gazed at the darkened windows of Lenore McCloud's house. It was nearly 2:00 a.m., and he'd been out here for more than an hour already. Waste of time, of course. No one was coming tonight.

He just needed to be here.

He wouldn't stay much longer. He'd head home in a little while, get a couple hours sleep. He hoped. More likely he would spend the rest of the night tossing and turning, just like last night.

His sleeplessness last night had been caused by that brief kiss with Deborah on her mother's front porch. He couldn't imagine what tonight would be like after what had taken place between them that morning.

Leaning his head against the back of his seat, he closed his eyes for a moment, savoring the memories of kissing her. Even as physically painful as those memories were.

He nearly came out of his seat when the passenger door was suddenly flung open.

"What the hell are you doing here?" Deborah slid into the passenger seat as she asked the question, slamming the door behind her.

"Damn it, you just about gave me a heart attack."

"Great police work, Smith. You never even knew I was here."

"I wasn't expecting anyone to climb in with me. What are you doing out here?"

"I saw your car from my window. But you never told me what you're doing. Surely you don't plan to sit out here on guard all night."

"No. I was just trying to figure out how someone

slashed your tires without any of your neighbors seeing anything. I figure whoever it was must have parked at the end of the street and walked to your driveway. Someone would probably have heard a car engine.''

''Not necessarily. It stormed most of the night, remember?''

''I doubt that anyone got out in the worst of the storm. More likely they showed up after the rain ended, probably just before dawn. It could even have been an impulsive move. Someone was out driving after the storm let up and saw your car, then acted out of frustration and anger.''

''Did you come up with any new leads today?''

''There are quite a few people around here with a grudge against your father. Not many are willing to speak badly about your mother or Isabelle. As for you, personally, you've been gone so long most people claim not to know you very well. I couldn't find anyone with a particular grudge against you. I suppose your car was just handy.''

''Great.'' She pushed a hand through her tousled hair. Just enough light filtered into his car for him to see that her expression was as disgruntled as her voice.

She wasn't wearing pajamas, but an oversized Buccaneers T-shirt, dark-colored leggings and flip-flops. She'd probably been to bed, but was as unable to sleep as he was.

He wasn't surprised she had recognized his car. He'd owned it for ten years, and she had spent quite a bit of time in it while they'd been together. They had cruised the town in this car. They'd made out up at Cutter's Point. They had even broken up in the car. He could still hear the echoes of the passenger door slamming behind her after she had ordered him out of her life for good.

"You still haven't thought of anyone who might have vandalized your car for a personal vendetta?" he asked, trying to keep his thoughts on present matters.

"You," she said promptly.

That made him chuckle. "As annoyed as I have been with you, I could never do anything to damage an innocent sports car."

She smiled just a little in return, probably remembering very well that he had always been a car buff.

And then she spoke again. "The only other confrontation I've had recently was with Kirk Sawyer—just a brief run-in. He made one of his sleazy come-ons, and I wasn't particularly pleasant in return. He left mad, but I don't seriously suspect him. Especially of the letter writing. He's not that literate."

Dylan frowned thoughtfully. He hadn't realized Deborah and Kirk were adversaries. Like Deborah, Dylan didn't think Kirk was the letter writer, but he could certainly picture the drunken jerk taking his spleen out on Deborah's car. "You should have told me this sooner. Maybe I'll have a chat with Sawyer tomorrow."

"You seem to be doing a lot of talking, but not much action. Other than lurking outside my mother's house in the middle of the night."

Draping his right arm over the back of his seat, he turned sideways to study her more closely. "Have you given any more thought to Lindsey's business proposition?"

"We aren't talking about my future plans. I asked about the progress of your investigation."

"And I answered you. I have no solid leads yet, but I'm continuing to pursue them. Now, what about your plans?"

"I haven't decided. Probably not."

"She'll be disappointed." As would he, but he knew better than to add that tidbit.

"She'll find someone else. It's a good prospect."

He thought there was some hesitation in her voice. Maybe she wasn't entirely convinced that she wanted to turn Lindsey down, but she was reluctant to think too seriously about it. Was it fear that held her back? Fear of failure? Fear of moving back to Honesty? Fear of *him?*

"I don't hear you talking about your personal business," she said, sounding defensive. "I had to hear about your book deal through the local grapevine."

He stared out the windshield at the darkened street. "There is no book deal."

"You've written a book, haven't you?"

"Yeah."

"And Adrienne's agreed to represent you?"

"Yes."

"Then there will be a book deal." Deborah sounded almost glumly resigned.

Dylan drew a deep breath. "Actually, I've gotten my first rejection. Adrienne called me about it when she and Gideon returned to Honesty this afternoon. The publisher politely declined to buy my book, then wished me luck placing it elsewhere. I'm sure that news makes both you and your brother quite happy."

Chapter Eleven

Dylan had tried to speak off-handedly, to sound matter-of-fact about the vagaries of publishing. He didn't want Deborah to know quite how disappointed he had been by the rejection. He hadn't even shared those feelings with his agent, choosing instead to put on a blasé front. Wryly humorous about the whole thing, even.

Since his youth, Dylan had made a practice of hiding his vulnerabilities. That had been another problem between him and Deborah.

But Deborah had always had a knack of seeing more than he had wanted her to see. She reached out to lay a hand lightly, fleetingly on his knee, a gesture of commiseration. "Every writer gets a few rejection letters. It's like a ritual or something. Much to my and Gideon's irritation, Adrienne will sell the book for you."

Dylan tightened his left hand on the steering wheel to keep himself from reaching for her. He continued to speak casually in an effort to conceal how much her reassurance had meant to him. "Yeah, maybe. It doesn't really matter."

"The hell it doesn't. If it didn't matter, you wouldn't have made the effort to submit it. When did you decide you were a writer, anyway?"

He studied his knuckles against the leather-wrapped steering wheel. "Not long after you and I broke up. I needed something to do to kill time, so I started scribbling. You remember that I used to do some sports writing for the *Honesty Gazette* in high school?"

"Of course. So you started writing again when you were living in New Orleans?"

"Yeah. I was working night shift at the docks. I never could sleep much during the daytime."

He'd spent too many of those days nursing a bottle of Jack Daniel's and a broken heart. The writing had kept him sane. His uncle Owen's intervention had kept him alive.

"So you've been working on this book for almost seven years."

"No. I wrote some real garbage at first. Took me about a year to write this one, once I decided what I wanted to write."

"Did you know when you started writing that Gideon was writing, too?"

"Didn't have a clue until after he published his first book. It was all pure coincidence, as bizarre as that seems."

"Not so bizarre, maybe," Deborah murmured. "Mother always said you and Gideon were very much alike in some ways. Lindsey made the same observation at lunch the other day.''

The very suggestion made him scowl. ''I don't think so. My books are nothing like Gideon's, not in style or voice or genre. And Gideon and I are nothing alike in any other way, either.''

''Funny. That's the same appalled expression Gideon always got when Mother said that to him. He said he would rather be compared to a—er—''

''Might as well finish it,'' Dylan said with a shrug.

''He said he would rather be compared to a wild pig.''

Dylan was amused rather than offended. ''Actually, I think I *did* compare him to a wild pig a few times. Among other things.''

''No doubt.''

''He's not too happy that I'm writing, even though I'm aiming for a standard detective series rather than the paranormal thrillers he writes. I think he still sees it as me infringing on his territory. Again.''

Deborah looked out the windshield toward her mother's darkened house. ''It must have caused some problems between him and Adrienne when you signed with her. Why did you approach her, anyway? Couldn't you find an agent who *wasn't* my brother's wife?''

''She wasn't his wife at the time. I didn't even know they were going to be married. And I didn't approach her, exactly. She sort of accidentally found out about my book and then pestered me until I agreed to show it to her. I never wanted to cause problems between her and Gideon.''

''Well, I suppose that's between the three of you. It's certainly none of my business.''

"No, I suppose it's not. But you needn't worry about me causing a rift between Adrienne and Gideon, Deb. I'll find another agent before I would let that happen."

He meant it, too. Adrienne was a nice woman. He wanted nothing but the best for her—even if the best, in her opinion, was Gideon McCloud.

Deborah nodded, then looked toward the house again. "I guess I'd better go back inside. And you might as well go home and get some rest. No one's coming tonight."

"Yeah." He cleared his throat. "Deb, about this morning…"

"I'd like to forget about this morning."

"You think you can do that?"

"I can sure as hell try." She sounded so grim about it that he was almost able to find some humor in it.

"Is there someone else? Back in Tampa, maybe?" It was a question he didn't want to ask, but felt compelled to.

She gave him a look that made him wonder if she would even answer. After several long moments, she said, "No, I'm not involved with anyone. I'm in no hurry to tie myself down. I like to be free to move around when I want to."

"No strings," he muttered. "Will you ever trust anyone enough to let him into your life again?"

"I don't know," she whispered and reached for the door handle.

He moved his hand to her shoulder. "Will you let me say one thing before you go inside?"

He felt the tension in her muscles beneath his palm. "If it's about this morning—"

"It's not. Exactly." Not that she was going to like this any better. "This is seven years too late, but I want to apologize for the things I said about your father that night. I was way out of line, and I've regretted it ever since."

He watched her throat work with a hard swallow. "As you recently pointed out, everything you said turned out to be true. I just didn't want to believe it then."

"I should have kept my mouth shut. I shouldn't have lashed out at you just because he'd treated me like dirt at your birthday party and you were mad at me for snarling back at him."

She shook her head. "It doesn't matter. That's all in the past, and I keep telling you I want to leave it there."

"I think we should talk about it. We never have."

She was shaking her head long before he finished speaking. "Don't."

He forged on, anyway. "I hurt you badly. I was young and stupid and so crazy in love with you that I couldn't think straight."

"So in love with me that you went out with someone else while I was away at college," she muttered, her face turned away from him.

"You know nothing happened between Carol and me," he said, impatience mingling with stirrings of old guilt. "I was angry and frustrated and feeling rejected by you and your family. I was beginning to think you and I would never make it work between us. I guess I was trying to find out if I could go on without you."

"I guess you found out you could."

"Did I?"

Before she could respond to what was basically a rhetorical question, he went on the offensive. "Besides, I wasn't the only one seeing other people. Every time you came home from college, all you could talk about was all the guys you'd been hanging out with there. Intellectual college men, not common laborers like me."

"I talked about my *friends*—of both genders," she retorted heatedly. "You only heard the male names. And never once did I imply that any of them were superior to you because they—"

She stopped and drew a deep, unsteady breath. "This is ridiculous. I'm not going to continue a seven-year-old argument with you. It's over. We fought, we both said cruel things and then we called it quits. I survived that night—barely—and I've made a good life for myself since. We both need to get over it and move on."

He drew a deep breath before blurting, "Or we could put it behind us and start over. As adults this time. Even you can't deny that there's still something between us."

She couldn't have sat more straight and tense if she'd had an iron rod down the back of her shirt. "It's called antagonism."

"Maybe. Or maybe that's just a cover for something more powerful."

She looked at him then, her expression heartrending in the shadowy illumination. "I can't do this again, Dylan. I almost died the last time. I won't ever give anyone that much power over me again."

"You could have a little more faith in me—in both of us," he said roughly.

Her voice was so low and thick that she didn't

even sound like herself when she said, "I just don't have that much faith left in me."

Moments later he was alone in the car, watching her hurry up the path to her mother's front door, obscured by shadows and then revealed again by the overhead security lighting. She never looked back.

He sat there a while longer after she closed herself inside the house, her voice echoing in his mind. *I almost died the last time.*

Why did he have the nagging feeling that she hadn't been speaking metaphorically?

Word of the McClouds' troubles spread quickly through the inner circles of Honesty society. Everyone was talking about it—though not necessarily to Dylan. It took both charm and patience for him to get anyone to open up to him about what had really been said behind the family's backs during the past months.

"I've never said one word against Lenore McCloud," Lucille Mayo declared emphatically. And then she added, "Of course, I did wonder how she could be so accepting of the child Stuart had with that girl half his age. I don't think I could have done it, myself."

"Do you disapprove of her accepting Isabelle?" Dylan asked, studying her expression.

"Oh, heavens, no. I think it's very admirable of her. Of course, she does get a little carried away with bragging about the child. I'm sure Isabelle is very bright, but my little Justin is quite special, too. Why, just the other day Justin did the cutest thing. He…"

It had taken him another twenty minutes to make

his escape from Lucille's monologue about her extraordinary grandchildren.

"You ask me, hon, Lenore McCloud's doing penance by having that little girl in her house so often," Carla Booker, a waitress at a local diner, remarked. "Probably blames herself for her divorce."

Dylan looked at the older woman with raised eyebrows. "Why would she blame herself? It was Stuart McCloud's affair that ended the marriage."

"Well, sure, but a man don't go tomcatting around unless there's something wrong at home, you know? I don't know Miz McCloud very well. She doesn't exactly hang out down at the bowling alley, you know? Anyway, she always seemed a little snooty to me. Money will do that to you, I guess—not that I'd know personally," she added with a cackle of laughter.

Dylan knew that Lenore had always been conscious of her social position, but she had been the one member of the McCloud family who had been unfailingly polite to him through the years. So, rather than responding to Carla's question, he asked, "How do *you* feel about the little girl?"

Carla shrugged. "I don't think about her one way or another. I'm not all that crazy about kids. Guess she's the McClouds' problem, you know?"

Joe Huebner's family had been residents of Honesty longer than anyone remembered. Joe's father had even served a couple of terms as mayor. Joe himself had retired from the electric company a couple of years ago. Not much went on in this town that escaped Joe's attention.

"I can't imagine who would have a grudge against Lenore McCloud," Joe confided to Dylan. "Far as I know, she never did anything to anybody. Now that ex-husband of hers was a different matter, altogether. He left a lot of bad feelings behind."

"Yes, he did. A lot of people around here felt betrayed when he pulled out of that campaign so scandalously."

"You got that right. Made us look like a bunch of blind fools for believing in him and putting our money into his campaign. Probably used it buying sparklies for his little chippie."

Now here was some anger. "Did you invest much of your money in Stuart's campaign, Joe?"

The older man shrugged, his weathered face grim. "Enough. And even more of my time. Spent hours helping out down at campaign headquarters. I thought it would be good for this town to have one of our own in the governor's office. If I'd known that Stuart was fooling around with that young blonde while I was licking envelopes, I'd have had a few choice words for him. As it was, I gave him a pretty good piece of my mind when the news got out and he announced his withdrawal from the race."

Dylan would bet Stuart had received quite a tongue-lashing from Joe when the scandal broke. But how long had that anger simmered in the man? "So, what did you think when Nathan brought Isabelle home with him?"

"I thought he had lost his mind," Joe answered bluntly. "Single guy like he was at the time, taking in a little girl who wasn't much more than a baby. I wasn't surprised when he married that pretty partner of his right quick afterward. He needed someone to help him raise that kid."

Dylan doubted that Caitlin would appreciate the

implication that she had been married as a live-in baby-sitter. "How do *you* feel about the little girl, Joe? Do you think Nathan was wrong to bring her here where so many people have been hurt by her father?"

Joe's snort belittled the question. "That little girl ain't no more to blame than the rest of Stuart's kids. Nathan was just taking care of his own when he took her in. Shows that he knows the value of family, even if his daddy didn't."

The investigation was still going nowhere. Had Stuart McCloud still been alive and had he been the one receiving threats, Dylan would have a notebook full of suspects. But no one out of the dozens of people he'd talked to during the past few days seemed to carry that grudge to Lenore. Either someone was a very skilled liar, or his leads were taking him completely off the path.

He almost called Deborah on Monday to report his progress—or lack thereof. When he realized that he only wanted to hear her voice, he made himself refrain from dialing her number. He doubted that she had anything to say to him that she hadn't said in his car.

Classes were letting out when he arrived at Miss Thelma's Preschool Monday afternoon. Several of the parents—some he knew, others he didn't—eyed him curiously when he entered the building in his uniform.

"Officer Smith!" Isabelle squealed in delight when she spotted him as she came down the hallway with her caretaker, the dauntingly efficient Fayrene Tuckerman. "Did you come to see me?"

He patted her head affectionately. "Not today, princess. I came to talk to Miss Thelma."

Though she looked fleetingly disappointed, Isabelle recovered quickly, flashing him one of her many-dimpled smiles. "That's okay."

He chuckled. "I'm glad you forgive me."

"Come along, Isabelle. We still have to go to the bank and the grocery," her companion urged.

"Okay, Mrs. T. 'Bye, Officer Smith. See you later."

"'Bye, princess."

He watched her skip down the hallway at the housekeeper's side, and he wondered again how anyone could wish ill on such a sweet child. Or any child, for that matter.

The school owner's office was at the end of the hallway. The door was ajar, and Dylan could hear most of the heated conversation taking place inside.

"I'm sorry, Mrs. White." Dylan recognized Thelma Fitzpatrick's blunt, deep voice. "But this really has to be my last warning. If Danny disrupts our school routines one more time, you're going to have to place him elsewhere. I still wish you would consider taking him to a counselor. I believe he's headed for serious trouble as he gets older."

"My son doesn't need a shrink," a woman insisted somewhat shrilly. "There's nothing wrong with him. You've just never liked him. He's too energetic and independent-minded for you. You want me to put him on those drugs that turn kids into dull little robots."

A long-suffering sigh was followed by, "Mrs. White, I'm not trying to turn Danny into a robot. I simply think a good counselor would help him learn to concentrate better and to exhibit situation-appropriate behavior so he can be successful in his school career.''

"I'll tell him to mind his teachers better, even though they all pick on him. But I'm not putting him on those drugs.''

"Then perhaps you should be thinking about other options for his pre-schooling. Because, frankly, I don't think your instructions to him will make any difference at all in his behavior. It's going to take more than that.''

Moments later, a woman stalked angrily out of the office, nearly barreling into Dylan in her haste to leave. Her steps faltered when she saw him, and she gave a quick, angry look back at the office, as if she'd had a sudden suspicion that Miss Thelma was having her arrested for non-compliance with preschool rules of order. But then she gave an impatient shake of her dark-rooted-blond head and moved on.

Dylan had seen the woman around town a few times, but he didn't know her. From what he had heard of her conversation with Miss Thelma, he was content to leave it that way.

"Officer Smith.'' The squarely-built, stern-looking school owner greeted him from her office doorway. "Please come in. As I told you when you called, I have only a few minutes available for you this afternoon.''

"I understand that you're busy, and I appreciate you seeing me.'' Following her motioned instructions, he sat in a straight-backed chair as she settled behind her cluttered but organized desk.

"What can I do for you, officer?''

Using as few words as possible, he outlined the

problems the McClouds had been facing and asked if she had any suggestions for who he should talk to next. "You know so many people in this town. I thought maybe you would have some insight for me."

Thelma frowned thoughtfully. "I'm afraid not, at least not immediately. I will give it some thought, and I'll contact you if any suggestions occur to me."

"Thank you. What about you, ma'am? Did you encounter any public resistance when you first admitted Isabelle to your school?"

She hesitated a moment, and then gave a short sigh. "As I'm sure you know, there was some controversy when Nathan McCloud first brought his father's daughter here from California. Lenore McCloud is very influential in this community, and she was initially very resistant to having Isabelle in town as a constant reminder of her husband's infidelity."

Clearing her throat, she looked just a bit sheepish when she continued, "To be honest, when Nathan first called to ask if he could enroll Isabelle here, I told him we were full. Lenore has been such a generous and active supporter of our school through the years, and I didn't want to appear ungrateful to her by accepting her ex-husband's child over her objections."

"What made you change your mind?"

"Nathan's secretary, Irene Mitchell, convinced me that I was being unfair to the child."

Because Dylan had met the forceful, intimidating Irene—twin sister to Nathan's equally scary housekeeper, Fayrene Tuckerman—he had to stifle a smile in response to Thelma's muttered explanation. He would have enjoyed hearing that conversation, he thought, before asking, "Have you regretted changing your mind?"

"Not at all," she said stiffly. "Isabelle is a bright and eager student who has been a real asset to our program."

"I'm sure it doesn't hurt that Lenore has decided to play an active role in Isabelle's life," he murmured.

Thelma's voice was cool when she agreed. "That has made everything more comfortable."

"And the other parents? Did anyone voice objections to you when you enrolled Isabelle?"

"There was some criticism at first," she admitted. "Before Lenore came around. Her longtime friends are very loyal to her, and they thought it was wrong of me to risk offending her when she's done so much for this school. But that changed after she decided to accept Isabelle. She made it very clear to everyone that Isabelle is a member of her family now and should be accepted as such. We've had several public programs this past year—Christmas and Valentine concerts, a spring play, an awards assembly—and Isabelle has been treated no differently than any of our other students."

"She gets along well with the other children?"

"Oh, very well." And then Thelma made a face and glanced toward the hallway. "Except for one little boy, I'm afraid. He doesn't get along well with any of the other children. As young as he is, just turned five, he's still very skilled at finding other children's vulnerabilities and hitting them there. Weight, appearance, clothing, grades, parentage—it's all fair game to him. He can be very cruel for a boy so young. But Isabelle handles his taunts as well as any of the other children do.''

She placed her hands on her desk then and pushed herself to her feet. ''I'm sorry to cut this short, Officer, but I have another parent conference scheduled. I'll be sure and let you know if I think of anyone who might be harassing Lenore.''

He wasn't particularly satisfied with the interview. Thelma had alluded to several people who had opposed Isabelle's enrollment, but she hadn't given him any names, and he didn't expect her to do so. Miss Thelma was very careful about maintaining a friendly relationship with the community.

The only thing he had really accomplished was to mark Thelma's name off the list. The woman was perfectly satisfied to have Isabelle in her school now that Lenore would be even more active in supporting the program.

As Dylan had expected, Kirk Sawyer was the least cooperative of everyone he interviewed.

''Yeah, I know the McClouds,'' he said, glaring at Dylan's uniform with an expression that made clear his disdain for the police in general and Dylan in particular. Dylan had written Kirk more than one traffic ticket, which Kirk always took as a personal affront, since he thought traffic laws were written for other people and not for him. ''It would be kind of hard to live in this town most of your life and not know them, wouldn't it?''

Dylan crossed his arms and studied the other man. A year younger than Dylan, Kirk had been the local football hero who had gone on to play for Mississippi State. He had spent four years after that playing second string for a pro football team until wrecked knees and a drinking problem had ended that career. He'd come back to Honesty to return to his role as football hero, because only here would he be treated that way.

Though officially employed by his father's successful automobile dealership, he spent few hours there, choosing instead to waste his days drinking, wreaking havoc in his sports car and chasing women—not all of whom wanted to be chased. He had just skirted being charged with assault on a couple of occasions, but the women who had complained about his behavior had never wanted to press charges.

Kirk filmed television spots for the car dealership, using his fading good looks and athletic reputation to make up for his lack of talent. Dylan didn't trust the guy any farther than he could throw him.

"Nathan McCloud was your attorney until recently, wasn't he?"

Kirk scowled. "I fired him. When a guy's constantly hassled by the local cops just because he's got some money and fame, he needs a lawyer who isn't so cozy with the town leaders."

Dylan knew very well that Nathan was the one who had ended the professional relationship. Nathan had gotten tired of defending someone whose only defense was that everyone was out to get him.

"Do you have any bad feelings toward Nathan?"

Flashing his best TV adman's grin, Kirk drawled, "I don't hold grudges against anyone, Officer. Even you. That takes way too much energy."

Dylan didn't return the smile. "How about Deborah McCloud? How do you get along with her?"

Something dark flashed through Kirk's blue eyes then. "I don't. Haven't seen her much in years. She couldn't shake the dust of this town off her shoes fast enough, could she?''

"I heard you had a little run-in with her the other day."

Deep lines carved themselves between Kirk's eyebrows.

Better watch out, frowning like that, Dylan thought. You'll have to start Botox treatments to smooth out the wrinkles for TV.

"I ran into Deborah at a restaurant the other day," Kirk agreed sullenly. "Tried to be nice to her, and she bit my head off. She never was what you'd call friendly, but I guess you would know that better than me. She pretty well put you through a wringer, didn't she?"

"Why don't you tell me how you feel about Isabelle McCloud?" Dylan asked, refusing to be drawn into a discussion about his history with Deborah.

Kirk looked blank. "Who?"

"Stuart McCloud's little girl. The child Nathan took in to raise after her father died."

"Oh. Her." Kirk shrugged. "I've heard about her, of course, but as far as I know, I've never laid eyes on her. Why?"

"Some people around here resent having Stuart's child in town as a physical reminder of the way he betrayed his supporters' trust. Not to mention what he did to his family."

"Yeah, well, some folks around here need to get a life. As for me, I couldn't care less if old Stuart fathered a dozen kids outside his marriage and Nathan chooses to raise all of them. I got better things to think about. Now, sorry to rush you off, Smith, but I've got a commercial to film this afternoon."

"Yeah, right. I'll leave you to get into your makeup."

Kirk's smile wavered, but he escorted Dylan to his apartment door without comment.

Dylan stepped out into the hallway, then caught the door with one hand when the other man would have closed it in his face. "Don't let me catch you driving drunk again, Sawyer, or you're going to be trading that sports car for a paddy wagon."

"Very clever, Officer. Did you hear that on a TV cop show?"

Dylan gave Kirk a hard look that made the other man's cocky grin fade.

"Just one more thing, Sawyer."

Kirk sighed gustily, looking bored. "What?"

"Stay away from Deborah McCloud."

When Dylan answered his phone Monday evening and heard Lenore's voice, he went instantly on alert. "Mrs. McCloud? What's wrong?"

"Nothing's wrong, Dylan. I'm sorry if I alarmed you."

"No, I just assumed…er, what can I do for you, ma'am?"

"I've decided rather impulsively to throw a surprise party for Deborah at the country club tomorrow evening. Caitlin and Adrienne are going to assist me. We've booked a room and invited family and friends and some of Deborah's old school chums. If you aren't on duty tomorrow night, I would like to invite you, as well."

Dylan felt his mouth twist. "I doubt that Deborah would want to see me at her party, Mrs. McCloud."

"Nonsense. You've been so kind and helpful to us

this past week. You've made yourself available to Deborah every time she has come to you for advice. I'm sure she's as grateful to you as I am."

He cleared his throat. "Perhaps you've forgotten that Deborah and I broke up on her twentieth birthday. My presence at her party would be uncomfortable because of that, if nothing else."

"That was a long time ago. Deborah is certainly mature enough to put a youthful breakup behind her. Besides, this is your chance to leave her with a pleasant birthday memory of you."

"I don't think—"

"I certainly don't want to pressure you into coming, Dylan, but I would love to see you there. Isabelle adores you. You're Adrienne's friend and client. And you've been wonderful to us this week. I never agreed with Stuart about you, you know. I always thought you were a nice young man, even if you had a little trouble with your temper when you were young."

He shuffled his feet on the floor like an embarrassed schoolboy. "Thank you," he said, not knowing what else to say.

"So you'll think about my invitation?"

Because he didn't want to be rude, he said, "I'll think about it."

"Excellent. I'll look forward to seeing you there."

"Oh, but—"

"I have several more calls to make. Goodbye, Officer."

He groaned as he replaced the telephone receiver. Lenore was a very gracious woman and he hated to disappoint her, but if there was one thing he knew, it was that his presence at the party would not be a pleasant surprise for Deborah.

Chapter Twelve

Deborah's birthday dawned cloudy, with the promise of rain in the air. She sighed when she looked out her bedroom window. Shouldn't twenty-seven feel younger than this?

Showered and dressed, she went into the kitchen where Lenore, of course, was already dressed for the day in a spring-weight twin set, a tailored skirt and pearls. Deborah's favorite breakfast was already prepared—Belgian waffles with freshly sliced fruit.

"Happy birthday, darling." Lenore gave her a hug and a kiss on the cheek.

"Thank you. Wow, this looks good."

A proud smile softened Lenore's face. Deborah knew her mother was happy because she was doing what she most enjoyed. Feeding someone she loved.

Deborah cut into her waffle as her mother set a

steaming cup of coffee in front of her. "What are your plans for today, Mother?"

"I'd like to spend the whole day with you. We could go to that art exhibit you mentioned the other day, have a nice lunch, then maybe see a film matinee in the afternoon."

It sounded like so many of her past birthdays, Deborah thought with a wave of nostalgia. Mother-daughter outings to art galleries and tea rooms and symphonies and movie matinees. Frilly dresses and lace-trimmed white socks. Evening birthday dinners with the entire family for Nathan and Gideon's little sister and Daddy's little girl.

"That sounds nice," she said, pushing the memories aside.

"Lovely. We'll leave as soon as you're dressed."

Actually, Deborah had thought she *was* dressed. She glanced down at her white shirt and khaki slacks. No pearls, of course, but perfectly respectable, anyway.

Since this, too, was a part of birthdays with Lenore, she nodded and murmured, "Yes, ma'am."

"We'll join your brothers for dinner at the country club this evening," Lenore continued. "They want to see you today. Oh, and their wives will be joining us, too, of course."

Amused, Deborah smiled around a mouthful of waffle and strawberries.

Maybe it wouldn't be such a bad day, after all.

The telephone rang, and Lenore moved to answer it. She sighed when she replaced it a moment later. "No one there," she complained. "I hate those computerized telemarketing calls."

Deborah laughed. "Not as badly as Gideon hates

them, of course. You at least answer your phone occasionally.''

''That's true,'' Lenore agreed with an indulgent shake of her head.

Half an hour later, Deborah reentered the kitchen, still wearing the white blouse, paired now with a slim, above-the-knee denim skirt and brown leather slide sandals. A fringed leather belt draped at her hips and she had added chunky turquoise earrings and a turquoise bead bracelet.

No pearls and no pantyhose—her mother would definitely notice the latter—but this was as dressed up as she was getting. Considering that a light rain had begun to fall outside, she thought she'd done more than was required for the dismal weather.

Deborah was smiling when she slipped into the kitchen. Her smile faded when she saw her mother hiding an envelope in the freezer half of the side-by-side refrigerator. ''You got another letter.''

Lenore closed the freezer door and whirled to stand in front of it as though to guard its contents. ''You look very nice,'' she said. ''Are you ready to go?''

She was too flustered even to have noticed the missing pantyhose—proof, as far as Deborah was concerned, that the freezing envelope held another disturbing letter. ''Let me see it.''

''Not on your birthday, Deborah.''

''That isn't important. We have to deal with this.''

''Can't we deal with it tomorrow? We have such a nice day planned.''

There was an almost plaintive edge to Lenore's voice, making her sound like a child whose much-anticipated school field trip had just been cancelled.

Deborah sighed. ''At least let's drop the letter off

with Nathan on the way to the art gallery. He can turn it over to Dylan for us."

Lenore's smile made Deborah glad she had proposed the compromise. "We can do that," Lenore agreed. "I refuse to let this wacko ruin your birthday."

As little amusement as she could find in the situation, Deborah couldn't help but smile briefly at Lenore's terminology. Gideon was the one who had dubbed the writer a wacko, and it was rather funny to hear the word uttered in Lenore's prim-and-proper voice.

Lenore wouldn't even allow Deborah to get out of the car at Nathan's office for fear that Deborah would become distracted by their outing. Instead, Lenore took the unopened envelope inside, making the delivery in less than ten minutes.

"Nathan said he would take care of it," she announced as she slid into the passenger seat of Deborah's car, closing her damp umbrella and placing it on the mat at her feet. "Now we can just put it out of our minds and enjoy the rest of the day."

Deborah fully intended to try to enjoy the day, but she doubted that she would be able to put any of her worries completely out of her mind.

She thought she managed to mask her concerns quite well for most of the morning. Unable to control her impatience any longer, she excused herself from the table at lunch and stepped outside to make a quick call from her cell phone. It had stopped raining, at least for a while. There was a damp chill in the air, but she didn't want her mother to catch her making this call.

Her first impulse was to call Nathan, but it was

Dylan's cell number she dialed. After all, she rationalized, Dylan would be able to tell her more about
the progress of the investigation than Nathan would.

He answered the call a bit curtly. "Officer Smith."

"It's Deborah."

"Oh." His voice warmed a few degrees. "Happy
birthday."

She couldn't help remembering that the last time
he had said those words to her was seven years ago—
a birthday that had come all too close to being her
last.

"Thanks," she said brusquely. "Did Nathan give
you the letter?"

"Yes."

"I assume you both read it."

"Yeah."

"So, what did it say? Same old garbage?"

"Pretty much."

Something about his guarded response made her
frown. "What was different about this one? I want
the truth, Dylan."

After a brief hesitation, he replied, "I would say
this one was much angrier. Enraged, even. Rather
than the usual single sheet of criticisms and veiled
threats, this was a three-page tirade about how unfair
it is that Stuart McCloud's bastard—the writer's
word, not mine—will be a valued member of Honesty society. From the way it was worded, you'd
think Isabelle was being named rightful heir to a
throne or something."

"Thanks for being up-front with me about it,"
Deborah murmured after a pause to digest his words.
She had half expected him to be vague and evasive
about the contents of the letter in an effort to shield

her from the unpleasantness. Maybe he assumed that Nathan would tell her everything, anyway.

"I just wish I had more to tell you," he answered grimly. "I've got to be honest with you, Deb, I don't know who's sending these things. No one at the post office has any clues, and none of the dozens of people I've interviewed have led me to anyone who has seemed particularly antagonistic toward your mother. It puzzles me why the anger seems to be escalating when your family has done nothing to precipitate it."

"Maybe that's why. Maybe the writer is getting frustrated by our refusal to acknowledge the demands or in any way comply with them."

"That's possible, of course. But I can't verify that without knowing who's sending them."

The discouragement she heard in his voice made her say impulsively, "I know you're doing the best you can, Dylan."

"Thanks," he said, sounding genuinely reassured. "I appreciate that."

"So what's the next step?' she asked gruffly.

"I'm spending today looking into people who might have a grudge against Nathan. People who have faced him in court on the other side of a divorce or lawsuit."

"I'm sure there are quite a few of those. I know of at least one acrimonious divorce he's handling now."

"More than one. He and I talked a while this morning, though we had to be careful about breaking lawyer-client privilege."

"I suppose I don't have to ask you again to let us know the minute you have a credible lead."

"Of course I will. In the meantime, try to enjoy

your day. Nathan said you and your mother have several nice things planned.''

''Yes.'' Oddly reluctant to disconnect, she added, ''Thanks for taking the time to catch me up.''

''I'll always make time for you, Deb.''

She could almost hear him wince as soon as the words left his mouth. ''Um, I guess that sounded a little corny,'' he added sheepishly.

Because it had—and because it had touched her, anyway, damn it—Deborah said hastily, ''I'd better get back to my mother. 'Bye, Dylan.''

''See you, Deb.''

She closed the flip-open phone—and then hit herself on the forehead with it a couple of times, ignoring the startled looks from passers-by.

Returning to the table, she laid her napkin across her lap and tried to keep her expression unrevealing when she asked, ''Have you ordered dessert yet?''

''Who did you call?'' Lenore asked perceptively. ''Nathan or Dylan?''

Deborah sighed. ''Dylan. But he had nothing new to tell us.''

Lenore nodded and reached for the dessert menu. ''Then let's finish our lunch, shall we?''

Deborah was as surprised as her mother hoped she would be by the birthday party waiting for her at the country club. Expecting to find only family around a dining table, she found a whole roomful of people instead, all eager to wish her a happy birthday.

The one thing that did not surprise her was that Lenore had given no hints of what was to come. No one could keep a secret better than Lenore.

Though she put on a credible show of pleasure,

Deborah's first reaction was less than enthusiastic. She wasn't really in the mood for a crowd nor for the unbidden reminders of birthday parties past.

It didn't take long for her to find herself drawn into the fun. How could she not be? Everyone was so warm and sincere in wishing her a happy birthday. There was laughter and conversation, good food and fine wines. And presents. Lots of presents.

Deborah laughed as she opened funny gag gifts from old friends and oohed admiringly over the real gifts from family. Though she couldn't attend the party because she was out of town on a sales trip, Lindsey had left a gift—a lovely glass-bead bracelet. The box was wrapped in pages torn from an office furniture catalog.

"Very subtle," Deborah murmured, setting the bracelet aside.

One gift remained, this one wrapped in pretty gold paper with a bow made of jewel-toned ribbons. "Who brought this one?" Deborah asked, searching in vain for a card.

Everyone just looked at each other and shrugged.

"I think one of the doormen brought that in," Adrienne said.

"You, um, don't think there's anything to worry about, do you?" Lenore asked Nathan in a concerned murmur.

"It isn't ticking, Mother," Deborah quipped, lightly shaking the package.

"That's not funny, Deborah." Lenore glanced around the room in apparent dissatisfaction. "I wish Dylan was here. I suppose he had to work tonight."

"You invited Dylan?" Deborah asked.

Lenore nodded, speaking for her daughter's ears

alone. "He was concerned that you wouldn't want him here, but I assured him you would be glad to see him. Especially since he's been working so hard on our behalf."

"Aren't you going to open the present, Deborah?" Isabelle asked, tugging at Deborah's skirt. "It looks pretty."

Moistening her lips, Deborah reached for the ribbon. She had a sudden, wary suspicion that she knew who had sent this particular gift.

She caught her breath when she opened the box and carefully lifted out its well-protected contents. The gift was a delicate porcelain carousel horse, its shiny brass pole rising from an oval wooden base. The detail of the piece was amazing, the white horse looking alive and proud as it tossed its chestnut mane and held its chestnut tail high. Tiny multicolored jewels glittered from its bridle and saddle, and one small black hoof was raised high in the air as if prepared to take a high, graceful leap. The gleam in the horse's dark eyes conveyed spirit and intelligence.

Caitlin seemed to be as enchanted with the figurine as Deborah was. "That's so pretty. What does the little brass plate on the base say?"

Deborah's voice wasn't quite steady when she answered. "It's the horse's name. 'Fearless.'"

"Oh, I like that." Caitlin reached out to stroke a fingertip over the horse's proud muzzle. "Was there a card in the box?"

"No. It wasn't necessary. I know who sent it."

"Is everyone ready for birthday cake?" Lenore asked brightly, perhaps sensing that Deborah needed the attention drawn away from her for a moment. They had already done the singing-and-blowing-out-candles routine, so the cake was ready for cutting. "Caitlin, Adrienne, would you help me serve, please?"

"I want cake!" Isabelle announced eagerly. "With a frosting flower on mine, please."

The controlled bustle that ensued gave Deborah a chance to collect her emotions. She placed the carousel horse carefully back in its box, then busied herself neatly stacking her gifts.

"Don't you want cake, Deborah?" Lenore asked. "It's strawberry, your favorite."

"Yes, I'll have some. I just wanted to set these things aside so they don't get knocked off."

"Are you enjoying your party?"

Forcing a bright smile, Deborah nodded. "Very much. Thank you for going to so much trouble."

"My pleasure, darling. I wanted to make sure you had a very special birthday."

"You always make sure of that."

Lenore reached up to touch Deborah's cheek. "You seemed to need an especially nice birthday this year."

Deborah wasn't sure how to take that, exactly. Had she seemed depressed to her mother lately? Because she wasn't depressed at all. A little tense, maybe, over the career decisions facing her in the next few weeks. Definitely unnerved by this thing with the "wacko." But not depressed.

To leave no doubt of that, she widened her smile. "Let's go have some of that cake, shall we?"

Maybe it was the single glass of champagne she'd had for her birthday toast. Or maybe it was a sugar rush from the rich strawberry cake. Deborah couldn't think of any other rationalization for driving to Dylan's house after the birthday party.

She had told Lenore that she simply wanted to go for a drive to wind down from the festivities. Other than urging her to drive carefully, Lenore had made no comments and asked no questions.

It was quite likely that Lenore knew exactly where Deborah was headed.

Deborah climbed out of her car as soon as she parked in Dylan's driveway. If she had hesitated at all, she probably would have lost her nerve.

She heard the dogs barking as she approached his door. Dylan was certainly aware that he had company, and she would bet he knew exactly who it was. Confirming that thought, the door opened as she approached it, and Dylan stepped into the doorway.

At least he was fully dressed this time. He wore a gray T-shirt and faded jeans with a pair of scuffed white sneakers. He looked more jock than cowboy at that moment, but just as appealing as always.

"Nothing else has happened, I hope," he said, searching her face.

"No. I just came from my birthday party."

"How'd it go? Were you surprised?"

"It was very nice, and yes, I was surprised."

"I'm sure that pleased your mother."

"She would have been even more pleased if you had been there."

He opened the door a bit wider. "Are you planning to continue this conversation from out there or will you come in?"

Smoothing her hands down the sides of her denim skirt, Deborah stepped forward. She had come this far; she might as well finish it inside.

"Want a soda or something?" Dylan asked after closing the door behind her.

She shook her head. "No, thanks."

Crossing his arms over his chest, he cocked one hip and studied her. "You want to fill me in why you're here or am I supposed to guess?"

"I came to thank you for the gift."

Dropping his arms, he hooked his thumbs in his belt loops, looking a little self-conscious then. "You knew it was from me, huh?"

She gave him a look. "I knew."

She and Dylan had met at a carousel. She had been riding it with a group of her friends, and he'd been standing there with a couple of other guys pretending not to watch them. He was the best-looking guy Deborah had ever seen with his shaggy dark hair and steel-gray eyes. She had pegged him as a rebel right away—a dangerous temptation for a sheltered sixteen-year-old honor student from a socially prominent family.

It hadn't been by design that she'd stumbled getting off the carousel, nearly falling right at his feet. But when he caught her in his strong arms to steady her and their eyes locked, she had known her life had just changed forever.

Okay, she'd still been young and romantic enough to think in clichés like that. But it had proven to be true, if not in the ways she had expected. Or hoped.

"Why didn't you come to the party?" she asked him now, the memories hurting too much to acknowledge.

He shrugged. "I didn't want to spoil it for you."

Moistening her lips, she asked, "What makes you think you would have spoiled my party?"

His eyes sharpened on hers. "Are you saying you wanted me there?"

She backtracked rapidly. "No, I didn't mean that. I just said you wouldn't have spoiled anything. There were a lot of people there. One more wouldn't have made a difference."

His mouth twisted. "As gracious as that sounds, I still think it's better that I stayed away."

She held her hands so tightly gripped that her knuckles cramped. "Mother and Isabelle would have been glad to see you there."

"It only matters to me whether *you* would have been glad to see me there."

She turned to look out the glass doors behind her, avoiding his eyes. It was dark outside and still cloudy from the rain earlier, so she couldn't see the lake. Mostly she saw her own reflection—her face looking strained and pale, her body stiff.

Dylan stepped close behind her and she watched his image come into focus beside hers. He placed his hands on her shoulders—an old habit. "Would you have been glad to see me, Deb?"

Staring into the panicked eyes of that Deborah in the glass, she swallowed. "I thought we had settled this already. I don't want…"

Her voice trailed off. She was having trouble thinking of the right words—or thinking at all for that matter—with him standing so close behind her.

"What don't you want, Deb?"

She didn't want to care again. She didn't want to trust again. She didn't want to be hurt again.

His hands kneaded, finding the knots of tension and working them gently. "Do you remember that carousel? The night we met?"

"I remember." Her voice was little more than a breath of sound.

"You were the most beautiful girl I'd ever seen. The way your blue eyes sparkled in the carnival lights. The way you smiled. Damn, your smile was amazing. Like the lights were inside you."

She closed her eyes, seeing that night again. The carousel, the whirling lights, the tall, gray-eyed teenager with the bad-boy grin.

"I don't see you smile like that anymore," he murmured. "I miss it."

"Maybe the lights have just gone out," she whispered.

Very slowly, he turned her around. She opened her eyes to find him gazing down at her, an expression on his face that made her heart ache.

Dylan didn't show his emotions easily. His childhood had consisted of being shuttled from place to place, never feeling safe or cherished, sometimes not even sure if he was remembered. Those early years had left him guarded and wary and uncertain. Maybe it was the reason he had been almost obsessive in their relationship, so afraid of losing her that he had driven her away.

She'd had a lot of time to think about his motivations during the past few years. As well as her own.

Maybe she had been a little attention-hungry because of her father's frequent absences. When he was home, Stuart lavished her with attention, spoiling her shamelessly. But he wasn't home often, workaholic that he had been. And Dylan was with her as often as he was allowed to be. Until finally she hadn't been sure she even existed apart from him.

"I can't go back, Dylan," she said, shaking her head. "I won't go back."

"I'm not asking you to." His warm breath caressed her cheek like a tender touch. "What we had before didn't work."

She slid her hands up his chest, leaving them to rest over his steadily beating heart. "What makes you think it would work this time?"

"There's only one way to find out," he murmured and closed his mouth over hers.

The kiss almost stopped her heart. It completely stopped her brain, replacing thought with pure sensation.

He moved his hands over her back, reaching down to scoop her closer against him. He was hard against her—everywhere. And she reveled in the strength that had always drawn her to him.

Murmuring her name, he kissed her again, his tongue plunging deep to mate with hers, making her ache for a more intimate union between them. This much had not changed, she thought vaguely. She still wanted Dylan as much as she ever had.

His hair was shorter than he used to wear it, she noted as she slid her fingers into it. Yet it was still thick and soft.

Again and again he kissed her, until she was warm and pliant in his arms, her mouth moving hungrily beneath his, her hands pulling him so closely against her that she could feel every sinewy inch of him. His arousal was bold and insistent as he moved her hips against his, making her shudder in response. Heat pooled inside her until she could hardly breathe, and she knew that only Dylan could ease the aching need that tormented her.

She wouldn't allow herself to fall in love with him again. But was she strong enough to push him away now, when she wanted him so very much, and when it was so very obvious that he wanted her, too?

"I can't," she whispered.

"You can," he murmured roughly. "Just for tonight, Deb, remember the way it used to be between us. The way it felt to be so strongly connected that we could almost hear each other's thoughts."

If he could hear her thoughts now, he would know that she had never felt that way about anyone else before or since. That she believed with every fiber of her being that she would never feel that way about anyone again.

Just for tonight, he had said. Could they do that? Could *she* do that? Pretend, just for one night, that the past seven years hadn't happened?

Dylan's hands slid between them to cover her breasts, his thumbs rotating over her nipples, making her gasp against his mouth.

Maybe she could think of it as a birthday present to herself, she thought as he swung her high into his arms, taking her silence as concurrence. A way to replace old, devastating memories with more pleasant, if bittersweet, ones.

And maybe that was nothing more than rationalization for something she wanted more than her next breath, she thought as he lowered her to his bed.

Chapter Thirteen

Deborah's better judgment might be shut down, but her senses were working overtime. Even though she refused to think about the past and its consequences, she couldn't help noting every detail that had changed about Dylan since the last time she had been with him this way. The new muscles, the new scars. The new patience he displayed in exploring her body, bringing her to new highs before giving in to his own needs.

His lips were warm and skilled as they moved from her chin to her throat to her breasts to her navel to her thighs. His hands were slow and clever as they followed the path his lips had blazed, lingering at each spot until she writhed helplessly beneath them.

When she could stand no more, he entered her very slowly, taking care not to cause her any discomfort, touching her so tenderly it brought a lump to her throat. It was she who escalated the rhythm, who urged him on with her hands and her body until the rigid control he had held over his emotions broke and his movements became almost frantic.

Just this one night, she thought before an explosion of sensation emptied her mind. Yet even then she knew that every detail of this night would stay with her for a lifetime.

Even before the adrenaline stopped pulsing through her veins, Deborah was out of Dylan's bed and reaching for her clothes.

His own breathing still heavy and uneven, Dylan lifted himself up on one elbow to frown at her. "You're running again?"

She concentrated hard on getting dressed. "I'm leaving. There's a difference."

"Not in this case. We need to talk, Deb."

"Talk won't change anything." Leaving her blouse untucked, she zipped her skirt and looked around almost wildly for her shoes. Where had she—oh, there they were.

Sliding her feet into them, she pushed her hair out of her face and risked a look at Dylan. Big mistake. He lay on the bed looking rumpled and sated, unselfconsciously nude and uncompromisingly sexy, a sight that started her heart racing again.

"I'll be leaving for Tampa early Thursday morning," she said. "Nathan and Gideon will be keeping a close eye on my mother, but I'm also trusting you to find whoever it is that's been tormenting her."

"You *are* running." Dylan rolled to sit up, reaching for his jeans.

Deborah refused to be drawn into an argument with him. She needed to get out of here. Now.

Okay, so she *was* running. Maybe Dylan should have sent her a horse named ''Coward.''

With a choked sound that might have been a low cry of pain, she turned and all but bolted from his bedroom, relieved that he didn't try to stop her.

Dylan had his jeans and shirt on before he heard his front door close behind Deborah. Shoving his bare feet into a pair of slip-on shoes, he grabbed his keys and hurried to follow her out.

He didn't like her leaving this late and this upset. Though he knew she wouldn't appreciate his protectiveness, he intended to make sure she got home safely.

He was in his car with the motor running before her car's taillights disappeared from view at the end of his road. Staying far enough behind her that there was a slim chance she didn't even know he was there, he kept his eyes on those glowing red lights.

He tried not to think beyond this self-assigned task of escorting her home. For sure he didn't want to think ahead as far as Thursday.

He had a little more than twenty-four hours to convince her to give them another chance and forget seven years of painful estrangement.

Expecting her to make a left turn onto the highway, toward her mother's house, he was perplexed when she turned right, instead.

He couldn't guess where she was going. This was the road that led around to the public access on the other side of the fishing lake. Not much out there except a few private residences and a couple of bait-shop convenience stores that would be closed for the night.

She drove very slowly, forcing him to brake to stay back. The road narrowed and wound around a few sharp curves, crossed a couple of concrete bridges and twisted again to the right. Though it wasn't particularly well-lit, Dylan knew this area well enough to drive it confidently. He was called this way often when reckless drivers missed a sharp curve or to disperse rowdy crowds of young people who gathered at the picnic areas after dark to drink, smoke and make out in their cars.

Up ahead of him, Deborah suddenly braked, bringing her car to a stop at the side of the road. Hell of a place to park, he thought with a frown, glancing at the sheer drop-off on the other side of the guard rail beside her. This was the highest point of the road around the lake, and there had been some deadly accidents here in the past when drivers had plunged their cars into the lake below.

Turning on the emergency flashers, he pulled his car in behind Deborah's, knowing she had to be aware of his presence now even if she hadn't been before. He watched as she opened her door and climbed out, moving to the front of her car where she stood haloed in the headlights, gazing over the guard rail to the lake below.

Unnerved by her odd behavior, he slid out of his car and moved toward her slowly, tensed in preparation for any sudden move from her. A cop's approach, he realized wryly. "Deb? What's going on?"

Though the night air was only mildly chilly, she had her arms crossed tightly around her, as if she were cold to the bone. "Why did you follow me?" Her voice sounded far away.

"I was concerned about you. I wanted to make sure you got home safely."

She didn't look around at him. "That wasn't necessary. I can look out for myself."

Based on present circumstances, he was reserving judgment on that. "What are you doing here?"

"Remembering."

The starkness of the word told him that they weren't pleasant memories. He couldn't think of anything involving him that had happened here, so what was haunting her now?

He wanted to touch her, but caution kept his arms at his sides. "Tell me."

She reached up to push her hair away from her face. "I almost died here."

He certainly hadn't expected to hear that. "When?"

"Seven years ago tonight."

Feeling as if he had just been sucker-punched, Dylan drew his hands into tight fists at his sides. He remembered her telling him that she had almost died the night they broke up, but he hadn't fully understood that she meant the words literally.

"What—" He cleared his throat. "What happened?"

She still wasn't looking at him, and her voice still sounded almost eerily disembodied, as if she had separated herself from the painful old emotions. "I sneaked out of the house late that night—well after midnight—and went for a drive. I still like to take long drives sometimes when I'm upset or can't sleep."

He remembered the night a week earlier when he had pulled her over for speeding after midnight. What memories had been tormenting her then? All he had known at the time was that he had looked at her sitting so spirited and defiant behind her steering wheel, and he'd finally acknowledged to himself that he'd never gotten over her. And that there was a strong chance he never would.

"I had cried myself half sick over our breakup, and I needed some fresh air," she continued without emotion. "I drove that bright yellow Mustang then, you remember. The one Daddy gave me for my nineteenth birthday."

"I remember." It had been the only one like it in town. Everyone had recognized Deborah McCloud's car.

"I drove aimlessly all over town for maybe an hour. Something brought me up this way, I don't know what. I had the radio on loud to block out my thoughts. I didn't want to think, and I wouldn't let myself cry anymore."

He could easily imagine how she must have been suffering that night. All he had to do was think back to his own pain. His own tears. "What happened here?"

She motioned toward the road ahead of them. "Someone came speeding around that corner on the wrong side of the road. I was caught completely unaware and almost blinded by high-beam headlights. I swerved to the side of the road. The other car never even slowed down. That was before they put this guardrail in, you know," she added conversationally.

His stomach lurched as he glanced toward the drop

on the other side of the sturdy metal rail. "You almost went over?"

"I brought my car to a stop with maybe an inch to spare. I think my right front tire was half over the edge."

"Dear God." He didn't even want to think about what might have happened. He wasn't at all sure he would have survived that night if she hadn't. Their breakup had been hard enough. Losing her forever, with no hope of ever seeing her again in this life, well, that would have been more than he could bear.

"You know what was the worst part?"

Squeezing the back of his stiff neck with one hand, he asked hoarsely, "What?"

"For just a split second, as I sat here staring over that edge at the lake below—I thought about hitting the gas. For just that one moment, I thought it would be easier to simply give up than to try to face the rest of my life without you. I wondered if maybe fate hadn't just offered me an easy way out."

Stunned to his toes, he stared at her. Of all the things she might have said, this rocked him most. The thought that she had even momentarily considered such a drastic act—because of him—was almost more than he could comprehend.

She continued before he could recover his wits enough to speak. "As soon as I could think clearly, I put the car in reverse and very carefully backed onto the road. I kept one foot on the brake so I wouldn't roll forward. I drove home very slowly, slipped into my bedroom and spent the rest of the night shaking like a leaf."

"You never told anyone?"

She shook her head. "Never. My parents would

have freaked out. I went back to college the next day, anyway. I told my family that you and I had broken up and that I didn't want to talk about it. My father and brothers were so pleased with the breakup that they didn't really care why, and Mother honored my wishes."

That sounded familiar. Dylan had never talked to anyone about the split with Deborah, either. He had just locked the pain inside, snarling when anyone strayed too close to it, leaving town as soon as he had the chance so he could leave the curious looks and nosy questions behind.

"You didn't get a good look at the car that almost ran you off the road?"

She hesitated before saying, "No, not really."

Dylan looked at her with narrowed eyes. "What does that mean?"

"I only caught a glimpse of it—I was trying too hard to keep mine from going over the edge—but it looked like Kirk Sawyer's car. He was home from MSU that weekend."

"That son of a—"

"I'm not positive it was Kirk," Deborah reminded him quickly.

"But you're pretty sure it was."

She shrugged. "I never liked him, anyway. He was always making heavy-handed passes at me—just like he did every other girl within range of his obnoxious attentions. After that, I could hardly stand to look at him, but I really didn't see him much after that night, anyway."

So that accounted for her antagonism toward Sawyer. Had Dylan known at the time that Kirk had been making passes toward Deborah, before Dylan learned to control his temper and joined the police force, well, Kirk probably wouldn't have walked away from that confrontation with all his pearly white teeth.

Dylan had been focusing on everything except what Deborah had told him about her fleeting impulse to drive off the edge of the embankment. Even though she had assured him she hadn't seriously considering following through on the urge, it devastated him that he had hurt her so badly the thought had even crossed her mind.

If it upset him so badly to learn about it seven years later, it must have been eating at her ever since. "Deborah—"

She turned to look at him then. "I only told you this because you followed me here. And because I want you to understand exactly why I won't let myself get involved with you—with anyone—like that again."

Because he could understand exactly what he and her father between them had done to her, he reacted with a touch of panic, speaking urgently. "You aren't a sheltered twenty-year-old girl anymore. You've grown up—we both have. You didn't leave me because of another girl, probably not even because of the things I said about your father. You left because I was smothering you. I understand that now. You needed to prove that you were strong enough to survive on your own, and you did that, starting right here on that night when you made the decision to save your own life. You've been proving it ever since."

She was shaking her head, looking as though she wanted to speak, but he rushed on, "I hurt you, Deb. Your father hurt you. But you were strong enough to move on and make a good life for yourself. I did the same. We both learned from our mistakes. We both know we can get by, but do you really want to spend the rest of your life alone? Because I don't—even if it means taking the risk of getting hurt."

"I can't, Dylan. Not again. Tonight was a mistake." She pushed past him, moving toward her car.

He caught her arm. "Deborah—"

"Please." Her voice was low, throbbing with pain. It hurt him to hear it. "Just let me go."

He dropped his hand. "I'll follow you home."

"That's not—"

"Just don't argue with me on this one, okay?" He was suddenly bone-weary, and he knew it was evident to her. "I'll follow you home."

She climbed into her car without another word of argument.

Lenore had plans for most of Wednesday. She was gone when Deborah was awakened by the phone ringing late that morning after another almost sleepless night.

There was no one on the other end of the line, though Deborah would have almost sworn she heard someone breathing. "Stop calling here, you pathetic loser," she growled, just in case it was the letter writer. "Get a life of your own, damn it."

She slammed the handset into its cradle hard enough to nearly break it in half.

She took her time showering and dressing in a pale-green peasant top and khaki-colored jeans. She took more care than usual styling her hair and doing her makeup. Anything to distract herself from her thoughts of what had taken place between herself and

Dylan last night. The occasional twinge of a sore muscle reminded her of their energetic lovemaking, but she wouldn't dwell on the memories, refusing even to acknowledge them.

Unable to spend the entire day alone in the house trying to control her thoughts, Deborah climbed into her car and headed for Gideon's place. She didn't want to spend too much time with Nathan today; her eldest brother was much too perceptive and much too obsessed with making sure everyone was happy. He would do everything he could to find out what was bothering her so he could fix it.

Gideon, on the other hand, would probably not notice that *anything* was bothering her. And even if he did, he would figure it was none of his business and that she probably wouldn't want to talk about it, anyway. Which was why she wanted to see Gideon today.

She knew he would be alone; Adrienne had left that morning for an inconvenient but necessary business trip to New York and wouldn't be back until Saturday. Gideon's house was outside of town, since her reclusive brother didn't like having other people too close to him.

Standing on his front porch, she rang the doorbell several times and then pounded on the door. She knew Gideon was home, but he tended to ignore phone calls and doorbells until the noise went on long enough to annoy him.

Finally, Gideon jerked open the door. His longish, toast-colored hair was all over the place, and he looked as though he had slept in his T-shirt and jeans. His feet were bare. "What?"

She smiled brightly. "I came to visit you."

"Go away. I'm working."

Rising on tiptoes, she kissed his cheek, making him grumble. "I'm going back to Tampa tomorrow. You have to be nice to me today."

Sighing gustily, he moved aside. "You might as well come in, then."

Fingertips stuffed into the back pockets of her jeans, she wandered past him into his entryway. "Got a cold soda?"

"You want to raid my kitchen, too?" He heaved another sigh. "In the fridge."

"Keep doing that and you're going to hyperventilate," she advised him, leading the way to the kitchen with Gideon following close behind her.

Pulling two cans of soda from the refrigerator, she handed one to Gideon and scanned the neat countertops. "Snacks?"

She thought he almost sighed again, but he stopped himself, probably so she wouldn't make fun of him. He dug a bag of cookies out of a cabinet and tossed them at her. "Here."

Catching the bag in one hand, she moved to the table. "Have a seat," she offered, taking one for herself.

"Thank you," he said dryly and straddled a chair on the other side of the table. "Now, what's up?"

She twisted an Oreo apart and took a bite of cream filling. Only after she had washed it down with a sip of cola did she reply, "I just wanted to remind you to help Nathan keep a close eye on Mother for the next few weeks."

"You hardly need to remind me of that. I'm the one who wanted to hire a bodyguard, remember?"

"Yes, well, you saw how Mother reacted to that suggestion, as I warned you she would."

"Yeah. But I don't care how much she protests, if these letters keep coming or get any more threatening, she's getting protection whether she wants it or not."

"It's reassuring to me to know that you're so protective of her. It makes it somewhat easier for me to leave."

Gideon took a swig of his soda. "So how come you have to go back tomorrow? You don't have a job to return to, do you?"

"Not at the moment. But I have to start lining up my plans or my savings will start looking pretty slim."

"This thing with Lindsey Newman, you're not going to take her up on it?"

She shrugged. "I'm just not sure it's right for me."

"From what I've been told, it sounds right up your alley."

"Yes, well…"

"It would be kind of nice to have you back in town."

The quiet comment made her blink. Coming from Gideon, that was practically a flowery speech. "Thanks, bro," she said, trying to speak lightly. "But I guess I'm just more comfortable out on my own. You should understand that."

He hesitated only a moment before saying, "Not completely. I mean, I like living out here away from the center of town, but I've never seriously considered moving completely away. This is home. Mom and Nathan are here."

"I never realized you felt that way."

"Then why did you think I stayed?"

"Laziness," she answered promptly.

He grinned crookedly. "There is that."

She ate another cookie half. "So, how are you getting along without Adrienne?"

He glanced at the digital clock on the front of his stove. "She's been gone less than four hours."

"I guess that means you're getting along just fine," Deborah said with a smile.

He shook his head. "Less than four hours, and I already miss her like hell."

Another statement of emotion from him. Marriage had apparently softened her brother.

"Wasn't it difficult for you?" she asked curiously. "Giving up part of your cherished privacy, I mean? Letting someone else move into your house?"

"It felt a little strange at first," he admitted. "But I don't know, Adrienne just seemed to belong here from the time she first arrived."

"And now, even though you're been married less than two weeks, your house feels empty to you when she's not in it."

He nodded. "Heck of a development, isn't it?"

"Doesn't that feel… I don't know…scary to you? I mean, what if something were to happen between you? What if she dumped you for some slick-talking New Yorker?"

"I'd kill him," Gideon said, reaching for an Oreo.

Deborah laid her hand over his. "I'm serious, Gideon. How would you feel?"

He scowled, but answered simply, "Like something inside me had died."

Releasing him, she crumbled a cookie on the table

in front of her. "Doesn't that scare the bejeebers out of you?"

"It did at first," he admitted. "I fought it like hell."

"And?"

"I lost. Thank God."

Another cookie crumbled into chocolate dust. "I wouldn't want to give anyone that sort of power over me."

"Does this have anything to do with Dylan Smith?" Gideon asked with sudden suspicion. "Because I don't give advice to the lovelorn, especially not if it means getting you together with that—"

"It doesn't have anything to do with Dylan," Deborah said hastily.

Gideon didn't stop frowning at her. "And I'm not talking about Dad. I don't do therapy, either."

"Oh, please, no." She was appalled at the very idea.

"So why did you come here?"

"I was hungry," she said, popping the last quarter of a cookie into her mouth.

"Oh." He reached for his soda can. "You're cleaning up those crumbs, you know."

Her eyes flooded with sudden, humiliating tears. She blinked them back. "I love you, Gideon."

"Oh, God. Here, have another cookie."

His appalled look elicited a watery giggle from her. "So tell me about your new book."

Gideon didn't usually talk about a work in progress—sort of a superstition for him. It was a measure of how badly she had unnerved him that he immediately launched into a detailed overview of his current plot.

Chapter Fourteen

Still not quite ready to return to her mother's house after leaving Gideon, Deborah drove aimlessly around town for a while. She would need a full tank of gas for the long drive back to Tampa tomorrow, so she pulled into a busy self-serve station. She had just stuck the gas nozzle into her car when she realized that Kirk Sawyer was filling his red sports car at the opposite tank.

The way he was glaring at her took her aback for a moment. Was he still this angry over her rude rebuff at the Mexican restaurant last week, or was it something else?

And then his scowl turned to an oily smile. "Well, hey, Deb."

She hated hearing the familiar diminutive in his voice. Ignoring him, she kept her gaze on the gas nozzle.

"I hear you're leaving town tomorrow," he went on, moving closer to her. Close enough that she could smell the alcohol on his breath even over the high-octane spilling into her tank. "Hicksville has gotten too dull for you again, I guess. After all, you aren't the pampered baby sister anymore, are you? Got competition in that area now."

"Get lost, Sawyer."

"And then there's your redneck-cop boyfriend," he added, ignoring her snarl. "I can see where he would get boring fast, although it must be a kick to your ego to have his tongue hanging out every time you come into his line of sight. 'Course, if you were interested in a real man—"

"I certainly wouldn't find one here," she cut in sharply. "The only guy I see now is a drunken ex-jock who doesn't know when he's just being pathetic."

A dark flush on his cheeks, Kirk made an abrupt move toward her, but then seemed to become aware of their very public surroundings. Muttering an expletive, he turned to his car, his unsteadiness evident. "Oh, by the way," he said as he climbed into the driver's seat. "Nice car. All new tires, I see. Better keep a close eye on them."

He slammed his door just as the words sank into Deborah's consciousness.

"Why, you son of a—"

She had her cell phone in her hand before she finished the curse, something she had been planning from the moment he'd approached her. She didn't call Dylan, but dialed 911, instead.

"Kirk Sawyer is driving drunk again," she reported to the dispatcher who answered immediately.

"He just left the Pump'n'Go station on Bender Street headed east."

She added a quick description of Kirk's car and license plate number—as if any cop in this county didn't already know it, she thought—and then hung up, satisfied that he would be quickly apprehended and hoping that no one would be hurt in the meantime. Maybe this time someone would finally get that jerk off the streets.

Her cell phone battery was going dead, since she had forgotten to charge it last night. She turned it off and stuck it in her purse. A short time later she found herself driving into the neighborhood where Nathan, Caitlin and Isabelle lived. It was almost three o'clock, so Isabelle would probably be home from preschool with the housekeeper.

She might as well stop in and spend a few minutes with the kid, she decided, turning onto their street. After all, she wasn't sure when she would be back in Honesty, what with changing jobs and relocating and everything. It could be several months before she made it back.

Liar, she told herself as she drove into Nathan's driveway. She knew very well that the reason she would stay away would have more to do with her cowardice than her work commitments.

She was rather surprised when Caitlin opened the front door in response to Deborah's ring. "Oh. I didn't expect you to be home. I just stopped in to say hi to Isabelle before I leave tomorrow."

"I had a free afternoon, so I came home. Isabelle and I are going to walk to the park. Why don't you go with us and you and I can talk while she plays?"

Though an afternoon at a playground wasn't her

usual form of entertainment, Deborah saw no reason to decline, since she was here, anyway. "Sure. That sounds nice."

Isabelle seemed pleased enough to find out that Deborah would be accompanying them to the park. "But you can't say anything bad about Officer Smith," she ordered, the only bone of contention between them.

"Isabelle, don't be rude," Caitlin murmured, holding up a finger in warning.

Isabelle sighed and hung her head, scuffing the toe of the little white sneaker she wore with her sunshine-yellow knit play clothes. "Sorry, Deborah."

"Let's just go to the park, okay?" Deborah casually ruffled Isabelle's golden curls as she spoke.

The kid was loyal to her friends. Deborah could hardly fault her for that. And she supposed it was nice that Dylan and Isabelle were so tight. After all, Dylan lived here in town where he would see Isabelle often. Unlike Deborah, who probably wouldn't be around much for the rest of the year.

Uncomfortably aware of a sudden hollow feeling deep inside her, she allowed Isabelle to take her hand as they stepped out of the house.

It was a nice afternoon, warm and fragrant, the air washed clean by the recent rains. Deborah felt some of the tension seeping from her muscles as they made the quarter-mile walk to the popular, neatly landscaped park. Even though it was a weekday afternoon, the beautiful weather had brought quite a few parents and baby-sitters to the playground with their young charges.

With a grin and a wave, Isabelle ran to join her friends on the slides, swings and jungle gyms. Deborah and Caitlin found an empty bench from which to watch her play.

"This is nice," Caitlin said. "You and I don't get to spend much time together."

"No, we don't. How are you this week?"

"Oh, I'm fine, for the most part. Nathan wanted me to take some time off after losing my mother, but I would rather stay busy working."

"I know. Staying busy keeps me from dwelling on unpleasant thoughts." She'd been staying almost frantically busy today, she added to herself.

"Exactly. And when I find myself getting down, I remind myself that my mother is in a much better place now."

Deborah watched Isabelle climb to the top of a slide with a little carrot-topped girl in a neon-pink shirt. Isabelle went down first, golden curls streaming behind her, her face alight with laughter. "Is everything else going well?"

"Oh, yes. The law practice is busy, with some very interesting cases. Including a medical malpractice suit that's been very challenging for several months now. I think that one may settle in my client's favor, which will be quite a coup for me since it didn't look too promising at the beginning."

"Good for you. So you don't regret turning down that offer from the big firm in L.A.?"

Caitlin's laugh was genuine. "Not for a minute. Here in Honesty, with Nathan and Isabelle, is exactly where I want to be."

"Not many women would have been so brave about giving up an offer like that to step into a ready-made family, especially considering the circumstances. Nathan taking in his little sister, I mean. And all the gossip that went along with it.''

"I don't pay much attention to gossip," Caitlin said with a shrug. "Unless, of course, it directly hurts my family, like this jerk who keeps writing to your poor mother. As for the ready-made family part, all I can say is that it has been a gift for me. I was so alone after my father died and then my mother had the stroke that took her away from me, too. I had almost convinced myself that my career was enough to satisfy me, but I finally realized that my work would never be a substitute for family. You've all been so welcoming to me. Even though I haven't been a McCloud for very long, I've really been made to feel like one.''

There had been a lot of talk of family today, Deborah thought with a frown. She was pleased that her brothers had found such devoted wives. That didn't mean that everyone was cut out for marriage, though.

Do you really want to live the rest of your life alone?

Shut up, Deborah silently ordered that nagging echo of Dylan's voice.

She frowned as she watched a stocky tow-headed boy push Isabelle rather roughly away from an empty swing. "Who's that?" she asked, as the boy climbed onto the swing.

Caitlin sighed. "Danny White. A real problem child.''

"Little creep just shoved Isabelle.''

"He's been a thorn in her side since she came here. I don't know why he torments her so much.''

Deborah watched as Isabelle and her red-headed

friend moved to a teeter-totter, instead. "I guess she has learned to ignore him."

"Pretty much. She had a rough time with him for a while, but Gideon helped her get past that. Both of your brothers are amazing with Isabelle, you know. She arrived a little subdued by everything that happened to her last year—her parents' deaths, her great-aunt's illness, the move here with strangers. She was very clingy at first and terrified of doctors. Nathan helped her get past both those hang-ups, and then Gideon taught her not to be so sensitive about what Danny and the other kids say to her. They'll both make good fathers."

The certainty in Caitlin's voice took Deborah aback. "You think? Even Gideon?" She couldn't picture Gideon with children.

"Oh, yes. I know Adrienne wants a child. Gideon says he's willing to discuss the possibility, but I think he rather likes the idea, even if he's a bit concerned about having his writing schedule disrupted. I told him he would learn to adapt."

Maybe he would, Deborah mused. It seemed that everyone in her family was better at adapting than she was.

She scowled when she saw Danny White run by Isabelle, elbowing her on the way past hard enough to make her stumble. Isabelle stamped a foot in irritation, then turned with her friend to walk in the other direction.

"If that kid touches Isabelle one more time, I'm going to make him wish he had stayed home to do homework today," Deborah said grimly.

"Nathan says Isabelle has to learn how to defend herself and we shouldn't be too quick to step in unless it gets serious.'' Caitlin shifted restlessly on the bench beside Deborah. "But I would love to put the fear of God into that brat, myself.''

Deborah could understand Nathan's point. Isabelle had to learn self-confidence and that came from learning to solve her own problems. But Deborah still wanted to flatten the little creep.

A familiar deep voice spoke from near the bench, causing both Deborah and Caitlin to look around. Wearing his uniform, Dylan stood close by, smiling at them. "I would say the two of you make a lovely picture sitting there on that bench, but I know at least one of you would not appreciate the compliment.''

Deborah was infuriated to feel her cheeks go hot, and she knew she must be blushing like a silly schoolgirl. The rest of her body felt uncomfortably warm as well, which she attributed to the sensual memories that flooded her mind at the first sight of Dylan.

Idiot, she told herself. You might as well wear a sign saying you're in love with the guy.

And that thought, of course, made her angry all over again. Who the heck said anything about being in love?

"What are you doing here?" she asked crossly. "Are you going to try to convince me that this is just another coincidental encounter?''

His smile faded, his eyes entirely too perceptive. "No, I've been looking for you,'' he said. "Mrs. Tuckerman said I could find you here with Caitlin.''

Tucking her hands beneath her on the bench, she looked away from him, embarrassed by her over-reaction at seeing him so unexpectedly when she had been working so hard all day not to think of him.

She focused on Isabelle, who was playing at the slide again and hadn't yet noticed Dylan's arrival. Deborah knew Isabelle would run squealing in their direction as soon as she spotted her beloved Officer Smith.

"Well?" Deborah asked without taking her eyes off Isabelle. "What do you want?"

Caitlin shifted slightly on the bench beside her, as if the palpable tension between Deborah and Dylan made her uncomfortable.

"I got a call this afternoon I thought might interest you," Dylan replied, strained patience in his tone. "I know who—"

Isabelle was on the platform at the top of the four-foot-high slide, along with her little red-haired friend and Danny White. There seemed to be a heated discussion about who was going down the slide first. Deborah was thinking about getting involved, despite Nathan's philosophy, when Danny suddenly reached out and gave Isabelle a rough shove.

He probably didn't intend to hurt her. Had she not been standing with all her weight on one leg, the other foot tapping in frustration, she probably would have been able to maintain her balance. As it was, she teetered, flailing her arms wildly, and then went backward head-first down the slide.

All of those observations went through Deborah's mind in the half second it took for the accident to happen. A heartbeat later, she was on her feet and running, watching with sick horror as Isabelle tumbled off the end of the slide and landed in a crumpled heap on the ground.

Dylan reached Isabelle at the same time Deborah did. Caitlin was right behind him, calling Isabelle's name. Chaos erupted around the slide, with children shouting and mothers dashing toward them.

As he knelt beside Isabelle, Dylan heard some woman take charge of the scene, calming the children and holding everyone else back. He would have to remember to thank whoever it was, he thought, before turning his attention to Isabelle.

The child wasn't moving. Crouched on Isabelle's other side, Deborah met his eyes. Her face was colorless, and her expression was a plea for help.

No matter how hard she had tried to stay detached from her little sister, Deborah had fallen under Isabelle's spell just as the rest of them had, Dylan realized. And she was frantic now.

His hand was amazingly steady considering his inner turmoil when he reached out to smooth Isabelle's tangled hair away from her face. He was relieved when he saw that her eyes were open and she seemed fully conscious.

Her lips were slightly blue and there was panic in her eyes. "Breathe, baby," he urged, resting a hand very lightly on her chest. "You're okay. You just need to take some breaths."

Her gaze locked with his, Isabelle took an experimental gasp, then grimaced with pain.

"That's right, princess. Breathe again for me."

Another jagged inhalation and then a sob. Isabelle burst into tears.

At least she was breathing, he thought even as he released the breath he had been holding in sympathy. As the color returned to the child's tear-streaked face, Dylan ran his hands gently over her little body, searching for injuries and finding none. She had hit the ground flat on her back with a hard, painful thump, knocking the breath out of her, but that was the worst of it, as far as he could tell.

A shrill voice penetrated his concentration. "Danny didn't do anything. He never touched her."

"Wrong." That was Deborah, and she sounded furious. "I was watching the whole thing and your kid shoved Isabelle down the slide. He's been pestering her ever since we arrived."

Leaving Isabelle in Caitlin's care, Dylan stood to approach Deborah, who was toe-to-toe with the bleached blonde he had first seen at Miss Thelma's Preschool. He hadn't even realized Deborah had risen to her feet. There was a familiar fire in her vivid blue eyes, and he suspected it was time for him to step in, before this confrontation got ugly.

Before he could intercede, Danny's mother—whom he now knew was named Cherie White—started shouting, "I am *sick* of you McClouds throwing your weight around in this town. You all think you're better than the rest of us, and you think just because this kid's got the McCloud name, she's better than the other kids. Well, I'm sick of it, you hear?"

Deborah stared at the woman. "What the heck are you talking about?"

"Like you'd know what goes on here," the other woman snarled. "You're too good to live in this one-horse town. You've got one brother who's a sleazy lawyer and another who's as weird as the books he writes. And your mother—"

"You really don't want to talk about my mother," Deborah warned, her voice very soft.

Dylan started to speak then, but something kept

him quiet, his gaze focused on Cherie White's flushed face.

"Oh, yes," Cherie snarled, her own eyes still locked with Deborah's. "Your saintly mother. The hypocrite who acted like such a martyr when your lying, skirt-chasing politician of a father ran off with that bimbo, and now your mother acts like their bastard kid is her own granddaughter. Pushing the kid down everyone's throats, buying her way into the best schools and social circles while the kids who really belong here are pushed aside. That girl has given my Danny nothing but trouble ever since Nathan muscled her into school, and now she's everyone's pet. Like the rest of us are too stupid to know it's because of the McCloud money."

Deborah's jaw had dropped during the diatribe, comprehension dawning on her face. "You're the one who has been writing those letters!"

Cherie White paled. "I don't know what you're talking about," she said, turning away. "Come on, Danny," she ordered the boy who stood nearby watching the commotion he had caused. "Let's go."

"Just a moment, please, Mrs. White." Dylan stepped neatly into her path, blocking her exit. "I would like to speak with you at the station for a few minutes. My patrol car is right over there. I'll have someone bring you back here for your car when we're finished."

She swallowed as she eyed his uniform. "What do you want? If you think Danny deliberately pushed that girl, you're wrong. I was watching him and he never touched her."

"Actually, he did push her, though I don't think

he meant to hurt her. Danny, from now on I expect you to keep your hands to yourself, you hear?''

Danny looked down at the ground and shrugged. His mother put her hands protectively on his shoulders. ''Don't scare him.''

Glancing at the boy's sullen face, Dylan thought privately that it would take a lot more than anything that had happened that afternoon to scare young Danny. Dylan would probably be seeing the boy again in a professional capacity if Danny didn't straighten up soon. And that was unlikely, considering the example his mother was setting for him.

''Come on, Danny, I'll let you see the inside of a police car,'' he said, motioning for the boy and his mother to accompany him. Probably won't be the last time you see one, poor kid.

Cherie scowled, hesitating as she debated between complying with his instructions and defying his authority. ''Am I under arrest?''

''No. We just need to talk, and I'm sure you would rather do so in the privacy of the station, rather than here in the park. Deborah, why don't you help Caitlin with Isabelle?''

Deborah looked at him in protest, still visibly shaking with stunned anger. ''But I want to hear what she has to say.''

''Deb—'' He spoke more forcefully this time, giving her a look that fell somewhere between command and request. ''Please leave this to me.''

She wanted to argue, but after a mental struggle he could read on her face, she nodded curtly and spun toward her sister-in-law, giving Cherie White a fuming look over her shoulder.

Dylan motioned again toward his car, and this time the woman and her son reluctantly accompanied him.

Isabelle sat cradled in Caitlin's arms, her cheeks still damp, her lower lip quivering. Deborah knelt beside them. "Are you okay?"

The child nodded. "Danny pushed me down the slide."

"Yes, I saw him." Though she knew both Dylan and Caitlin had checked Isabelle for injuries, she couldn't resist reaching out to feel the back of Isabelle's head. No bumps that she could detect. "You didn't hit your head?"

"I don't think so. I hit my back. Caitlin said I knocked my breath out."

"I'm sorry. That had to hurt."

Isabelle sniffed and nodded, then looked up at Caitlin, "I think ice cream would make it better."

Caitlin gave a shaky laugh and kissed the top of Isabelle's head. "You think ice cream makes *everything* better."

Isabelle's lips curved into a hint of her usual smile. "So does Officer Smith. But he likes butter pecan and I don't."

Deborah looked toward the curb where the patrol car had been. She was still a bit annoyed with Dylan for not letting her hear this discussion, but she supposed the park wasn't the right place for an official interview. She met Caitlin's eyes over Isabelle's head. "Did you hear any of that?"

Caitlin nodded. "She's the one, isn't she?"

"Apparently."

"Do you think Dylan already knew? He said he tracked us here to tell us something."

"I don't know." She could only assume Dylan would be home soon to fill her in. "We'd better go. I bet you've got ice cream at your house, don't you?"

"Of course. And Isabelle may have a scoop—after dinner," Caitlin added with a smile.

Deborah watched Isabelle get up and brush the dirt off her clothes, satisfying herself that the child was moving comfortably. She had wondered if they should take Isabelle to a doctor, but Caitlin seemed to think everything was okay.

They had made it only halfway back to the house when Isabelle complained of being tired. Deborah promptly swung the child into her arms. Though she looked a bit startled, Isabelle wrapped her arms trustingly around Deborah's neck. Deborah was almost surprised by how little the child weighed; she really was just a tiny little thing.

Deborah's heart still skipped a beat when she remembered the moment when Isabelle had tumbled backward. Her arms tightened a bit convulsively around Isabelle's little body as the scene replayed itself again and again in her head.

Don't get close. Don't risk getting hurt. It had been a good motto all these years. But apparently it had abandoned her. She had gotten attached, and it would have hurt horribly if Isabelle had been seriously injured.

She left Caitlin's house in a pensive mood, promising to call as soon as Dylan filled her in. Deborah had a lot to do that evening. She hadn't even started packing yet.

She really was ready to leave Honesty, she assured herself, despite the slight depression that accompanied the thought. She had things to do in Tampa.

Plans to make. There was no reason at all for her to stay here in Honesty, except to make sure everyone would be okay after she left.

Everyone, perhaps, except her.

Chapter Fifteen

Because she wanted to make certain she had been right about solving the letter writer's identity, Deborah didn't mention her suspicion to her mother. She did tell Lenore about Isabelle's accident, because she knew Lenore would hear about it, anyway. Even though Deborah assured her Isabelle would be fine, Lenore had to rush to the phone to call Caitlin, just to check for herself.

Family, Deborah thought with a shake of her head. All in all, it was exhausting.

She paced while Lenore was on the phone, waiting for the doorbell. Dylan should be there at any time. He knew she was impatient to hear everything.

"Are you expecting someone?" Lenore asked, entering the living room to find Deborah moving from one window to another, watching for Dylan's car.

"Dylan should be stopping by soon to let us know how his investigation is going."

"Oh. Then I'd better put on a fresh pot of coffee. I made those brownies last night, and I still have more than half the batch left. He'll like those."

Deborah sighed. "It won't be a social call, Mother. This is his business."

"That doesn't mean we can't be hospitable. Dylan likes my cooking. Myra Smith is a dear woman, of course, but she's never been much of a baker."

"Nobody in this town bakes better than you do, Mother. But—"

"I'll go start the coffee."

Lenore disappeared before Deborah could make another objection. She sighed and looked out the window again. It wouldn't surprise her a bit if Lenore invited Dylan over for coffee and baked goods quite frequently once this was all over. Between his business association with Adrienne, his friendship with Isabelle and his admiration of her mother, Dylan was rapidly becoming another member of the family. He would probably see them all more than Deborah did.

Her stomach was starting to hurt. She pressed a hand against it. Maybe she was hungry, too.

When the doorbell finally rang, she was caught unprepared since she had moved away from the windows to pace the room. She bolted for the front door, throwing it open before he could buzz again.

Dylan looked tired, she noted immediately. There was no gleam of satisfaction in his eyes, no cocky angle to his chin. She frowned. "Well? Was she the one?"

"Yes." He glanced past her into the living room. "May I come in?"

"Oh. Of course."

It bothered her that he looked so dispirited. The interview with Danny White's mother must have been trying. "Mother's making coffee and serving brownies," she said in an attempt to cheer him up.

His smile didn't reach his eyes. "Just as well this case is solved. Every time I come over, your mom feeds me something fattening."

"Tell me about it. I always have to diet for a month after a visit home."

He ran his gaze slowly down her body. "You hardly need to diet."

Clearing her throat, she motioned him to a chair. "I'll tell Mother you're here. Oh, here she is."

Lenore was actually carrying a tray when she entered, on which she balanced three cups of coffee and three dessert plates of brownies. Dylan reached out quickly to relieve her of the load and set it on the coffee table for her. "This looks delicious."

Lenore waited until everyone was served and seated before asking, "How's your family, Dylan? Is everyone well?"

"Very well, thank you."

Deborah had no intention of letting them get distracted by idle chatter. "Tell us what you found out, Dylan."

Lenore gave her a look that chided her for her curtness, but Deborah focused on Dylan. He took a sip of his coffee, then began. "I received a call this afternoon from Thelma Fitzpatrick. She said she had received a disturbing letter and she thought I should see it."

Lenore looked distressed. "Oh, dear. Miss Thelma is receiving the letters, too?"

"Only the one. And this one was signed. It seems that Thelma removed a troublesome child from her school yesterday after repeated warnings to his mother met with no response."

"Danny White," Deborah said without hesitation.

Dylan nodded. "Danny's mother, Cherie White, wrote a long, angry letter of protest, threatening lawsuits and boycotts and all sorts of trouble for the school. She mentioned Isabelle several times in the diatribe, saying her son hadn't had problems at school until Isabelle came—a claim Thelma assured me is completely inaccurate. She made wild accusations about money and influence and called Thelma a coward for taking Isabelle in against her better judgment."

"It sounds very much like the letters I've been receiving," Lenore observed.

"I took one of those letters with me. The handwriting was identical. I had no doubt Cherie White had been writing to you."

"And that's when you came looking for me?" Deborah asked him.

He nodded. "I tried your cell phone, but you didn't have it on. I made a few other calls and ending up getting through to Mrs. Tuckerman, who told me where I could find you. I didn't know Cherie White would be at the park, too, though she told me at the station that she goes there often. She made it clear she considers Isabelle the interloper there."

"So she admitted to writing the letters?" Deborah asked.

"Not at first, of course. She denied it vehemently until I set the letters in front of her next to the one she wrote to Thelma. Then she went on the offensive,

verbally attacking your family again, accusing the
McClouds of waging a campaign to have her Danny
expelled from the school just because Isabelle doesn't
like him.''

"Well, that's just nonsense," Lenore said.

"Yes, ma'am, I know. I'm afraid the woman has
some emotional problems. It seems her husband left
her for another woman about the same time your
marriage broke up, leaving her with an infant son to
raise on her own. She works part-time at a grocery
store to support him, along with help from her parents
and occasional, unreliable child-support checks from
her ex-husband. Isabelle is a symbol of everything
she so bitterly resents. She sees Isabelle as direct
competition to her spoiled and difficult son.''

"She must be under a great deal of stress," Lenore
murmured with a note of sympathy that made Deborah's blood pressure rise.

"Surely you aren't feeling sorry for the woman,
Mother. She has tormented you with those letters, and
she allows her brat of a son to bully the other kids
at school, especially Isabelle.''

"And there is the matter of ruining your tires,"
Lenore added sadly. "That went well over the line,
I'm afraid.''

"She still denies doing that, by the way," Dylan
said. "Even after she admitted writing the letters, she
said she had nothing to do with the tires.''

Deborah shook her head, remembering her alter-
cation with Kirk. "I don't think she had anything to
do with my tires. I think it was Kirk Sawyer. I can't
prove it, but I really believe he did it.''

"I think you're right," Dylan said.

Telling Lenore they would talk about Kirk later,

Deborah went on, ''I still think Cherie should probably go to jail for harassment or mailing threatening letters or something.''

''And leave her little boy without a mother?'' Lenore frowned and shook her head. ''I would rather see her get counseling. For both of them, actually.''

''Another idea I suggested to her,'' Dylan agreed. ''She was resistant at first, but I made it clear that her recent behavior will not be tolerated and that she is in danger of losing her son if she doesn't get help. My uncle will make sure there is proper follow-up.''

Deborah muttered, ''As long as she stays away from my family—*all* of my family—in the future.''

When neither Lenore nor Deborah had any more questions to ask of Dylan, Lenore stood. ''I want to call Nathan and Gideon and tell them about this. I'll probably be a while, since I'm sure they'll both have many questions. Thank you again, Dylan.''

''You're welcome, ma'am. You be sure and call me if there's ever any more trouble, okay?''

''I will. Deborah, make sure he has another cup of coffee and another brownie before he leaves. And, Dylan, stop by and see me sometime. You don't have to have a professional excuse to visit, you know.''

Deborah got the distinct impression that Lenore was deliberately leaving her alone with Dylan. Surely her mother wasn't making a clumsy attempt at matchmaking.

An awkward silence lingered in Lenore's absence. ''Good brownies,'' Dylan said finally.

''Would you like another one?''

''No, thanks.''

He looked weary again as he set his empty coffee cup aside. Deborah supposed he hadn't had much more sleep than she had lately. He would probably be relieved when she was no longer causing him so much trouble, she thought, noticing that hollow ache that she had futilely tried to write off as hunger.

"I guess you're relieved that we've found the person responsible for the letters," he said. "I know you were concerned about leaving it in question."

"Yes, I was." She wondered why she wasn't feeling more satisfied. She supposed she had been through such an emotional wringer in the past few days that she hardly had any strength left for more.

Dylan stood and moved restlessly around the room. "So you're still leaving first thing in the morning?"

"I'll try to get away before noon. I've been too keyed up to pack today—worried about the letters situation, of course."

He hooked his thumbs in his belt, looking uncharacteristically uncertain. "Any chance I can talk you into having dinner with me tonight?"

"I don't think that's a good idea, Dylan. There's really nothing left for us to say to each other."

"I can think of a few more things *I* want to say," he replied roughly.

She swallowed. "It wouldn't serve any purpose."

"So that's it? The case is over, the past put to rest and you're moving on?"

Unable to sit any longer, herself, she sprang to her feet, locking her arms around herself. "That sums it up pretty well."

He muttered a curse and turned to pace the other direction. "The one thing I never thought you were was a coward."

Her mouth twisted. "I know. Fearless. That's what you called me back then. The name you had inscribed on the carousel horse. But it's wrong, you know. I've never been fearless where you were concerned. When we were together, I was always afraid of losing you. After we broke up, my biggest fear became ever being hurt like that again."

"If you would just have a little faith in me. In us...."

She turned her face away from him, unable to answer. It was all too much for now, she thought. Too much emotion. Too much fear. Too much need. She wanted to hide somewhere in solitude and rebuild her battered emotional barriers. "I'll walk you to the door."

He wanted to argue. He wanted to grab her and shake her—or kiss her—into compliance. She could see those urges in his expression, in the taut set of his shoulders. And for just a moment, she thought he might give in to at least one of them. But then his shoulders relaxed and he nodded glumly.

She opened the front door and he started to move through it. He stopped halfway out to turn toward her. Before she could predict the move, he reached out to catch her chin with one hand, his mouth covering hers in a kiss as angry as it was passionate. She was shaking like a leaf by the time he finally released her.

"For the record," he said, his voice sandpaper-rough, "I have never stopped loving you."

And then he was gone, slamming the door behind him with a sound that mimicked the shattering of Deborah's fragilely patched heart.

Sometime later, Lenore found Deborah sitting on the couch, her arms still locked around her middle, rocking in misery.

"Oh, Deborah." Lenore stroked her hair as she sat down beside her. "Why do you always have to fight so hard against being happy?"

Deborah shook her head. "I can't give in to Dylan again. I can't risk being hurt the way I was before. You don't understand, Mother."

"And that is a very self-absorbed thing for you to say." Lenore's voice was firm, if sympathetic. "What on earth makes you think I wouldn't know how badly you suffered when you and Dylan broke up? How could I not understand when I went through it myself such a short time later?"

Wincing, Deborah said, "I'm sorry. Of course you know. So you *do* understand why I can't take a risk like that again. It would be foolish and self-destructive on my part, and I like to think I'm neither of those things."

"Or maybe you're being foolish and self-destructive to walk away from the man you have always loved with all your heart," Lenore countered gently.

Deborah gulped in panic at hearing the truth stated so calmly. "You loved Daddy, too. Look what that got you."

Her mother drew a deep breath, as if struggling for patience. "Dylan is not Stuart. They aren't anything alike. Yes, I loved Stuart, but I was never blind to his shortcomings. Dylan has flaws of his own, being only human, but lack of loyalty is not one of them. After all these years, he still loves you, anyone can see that."

Deborah swallowed hard. "Maybe. But that doesn't guarantee anything."

"Life doesn't offer guarantees, my darling. I thought I'd taught you that. Even had I known how my marriage to Stuart would end, I wouldn't have changed a thing. My marriage left me with years of happy memories and a wonderful family to give me love and companionship for the rest of my life. I would hate to see you miss out on those things just because you've had some heartaches along the way thus far. Don't let Stuart ruin your future the way he almost shattered this family, Deborah."

"I'm scared," Deborah whispered, years of pent-up tears coursing down her cheeks. "I'm really scared, Mom."

Lenore gathered her into her arms. "I know you are, darling. It takes a great deal of faith to give your heart to anyone. But I think Dylan could well be worth the risk, don't you?"

Lights burned in the windows of Dylan's shabby but neat mobile home at eight o'clock Thursday evening. The two goofy-looking dogs raced in their pen, their eyes glittering in the overhead security lighting, their tails wagging as they did their job of announcing a visitor.

Climbing slowly out of her car, Deborah smoothed her damp palms down the sides of the gauzy print skirt she wore with a silky black scoop-necked T-shirt. She had never been this scared in her life.

Dylan had the door open by the time she moved onto his bottom step. He had changed out of his uniform, she noted as she gazed up at him. He wore a red polo shirt now with a pair of dark jeans. His hair was still damp from a shower and he was clean-shaven, though there were dark circles beneath his eyes and deep lines carved around his mouth.

"Were you going out?" she asked him.

"I was thinking about coming after you," he admitted, his hands hooked in his belt as if to keep them from reaching for her. His voice was low and tight. "I've picked up my car keys a half dozen times. I had just picked them up again when I heard your car."

She dampened her lips, somehow encouraged to hear that he hadn't been prepared to let her go without making one more attempt to change her mind. "There's something I need to say to you."

"Aren't you coming in?"

"Not yet." She clutched the banister tightly, taking a deep breath. "I want you to understand that even if you and I are together, I have to remain my own person. I'll make my own business decisions. My own friends. I won't be an extension of you, with my happiness totally dependent on you. The way I was before."

Illuminated by the porch light beside him, Dylan's expression managed to be hopeful and irritated all at one time. "I don't expect you to be an extension of me. I don't even want that. I never did. Your independent spirit was one of the things I always admired most about you. You *are* your own person, Deb. I know nothing about your business, though I'd like to hear all about it. I have friends of my own. A career of my own—maybe a new career getting started. Who knows? The point is, I can get by without you, just as you can get by without me. Maybe even be happy, for the most part. But I believe without any doubt that we can be happier together.''

He had so much faith in them. It was time for Deborah to take that leap, herself, letting herself really trust someone for the first time in seven very long years. Though she took another step upward on the short staircase, she felt more as though she had just taken a blind jump off a tall, scary cliff.

''For the record,'' she said as he waited with barely restrained impatience for her to join him, ''I never stopped loving you, either.''

His arms were open when she reached the top step. Without hesitation, she walked into them. As they closed tightly around her, she realized that she had finally come home.

He drew her inside, closing the door behind them. His mouth was already on hers, his hands racing hungrily over her, as if to reassure himself that she was really there.

Her own hands were as recklessly demanding. She ached for him, and she was ready to show him exactly how much she had always wanted him. How much she loved the boy he had been and the man he had become.

With a gasp, he broke off the kiss and cupped her face in his hands, looking down at her with an emotion that brought tears to her eyes yet again. It had always been so hard for Dylan to share his feelings, so difficult for him to overcome the rejections from his past. To trust anyone enough to let them see the real Dylan. Apparently, it had become easier for him now, at least with her.

''You're sure, Deb?'' he asked gruffly, anxiously searching her eyes.

"I'm sure." It was less difficult to say it this time. "I love you, Dylan. With all my heart."

"I love you, too." He kissed her again, his tongue plunging deep to mate with hers.

He took her right to the edge of madness again before abruptly dropping her back to earth. "I'll be right back," he said, dashing from the room.

Stunned and disoriented, Deborah pushed her hair out of her eyes, wondering what on earth he was doing. She was beginning to think she was the one who was going to have to drag *him* off to bed.

When he reappeared, he was wearing another intense expression and carrying a small, silver-wrapped present with a rather ragged white bow. "I have a birthday present for you," he said.

She caught an unsteady breath. "You already gave me a present."

"That was for this year." Moving to stand very close to her, he looked deeply into her eyes. "I bought this one for your twentieth birthday, but everything fell apart between us before I could offer it to you. You weren't ready to receive it then, and truth be told, maybe I wasn't really ready, either. But we've done a lot of growing up since then, and I think we're ready now. I hope you agree."

She hesitated for several long, almost paralyzed moments. He was offering much more than whatever was inside this box, she realized. He was offering his heart. And by accepting it, she had to give him hers in return.

It turned out to be an easy trade, after all. She took the box from his hands, hearing him release a low, deep breath of relief.

The ring was beautiful. The brilliant round diamond was set in gold, and it must have cost him everything he had made on his construction job that year. How long had he made payments on it after she had left him? How much faith had it taken for him to keep it all this time, hoping someday he could give it to her?

"Yes," she whispered, slipping the ring from the box that had protected it for those tumultuous years.

"I haven't asked yet," he reminded her, a shaky note of amusement in his voice.

"The answer is still yes. You're right, I wasn't ready then. I am now."

The box fell to the floor along with its faded wrapping when Dylan swept her into his arms. She held the ring tightly in her left hand to keep from dropping it.

His mouth on hers, Dylan turned to carry her to the bedroom.

Deborah hadn't forgotten the past. She hadn't completely recovered from the wounds that had been inflicted on her. She hadn't reached Nathan's or Lenore's or even Gideon's level of forgiveness for Stuart's ultimate betrayal. But maybe she would get there someday. She had a loving, close-knit family to help her learn how.

A family that included Dylan now.

Her arms locked tightly around his neck, Deborah finally understood that it was possible for two distinctly different individuals to share one heart.

Epilogue

Isabelle McCloud looked happily around the roomful of family and friends gathered around Lenore's dining-room table on a very nice evening in late September. The table itself almost groaned beneath the bounty of food Lenore had prepared for her dinner party, and there was laughter in this house that had survived so much pain.

"I sure have a lot of brothers and sisters now," Isabelle said in wonder, looking at Deborah and Dylan, who sat across the table from her.

Isabelle, of course, was delighted that she could call Dylan her brother now. And Nathan and Gideon were slowly getting used to the idea, Deborah thought with a wry smile, though it was taking Gideon a bit longer than Nathan to adjust. But since even Gideon had to admit how happy Deborah was now that she and Dylan were back together, he had agreed to set aside his old grudges for his sister's sake.

"I would like to make a toast," Lenore said impulsively, rising to her feet at the head of the table with a glass of iced tea in her hands.

Though her offspring looked at her a bit quizzically, everyone obligingly reached for their own glasses, Isabelle's holding milk.

"First to Isabelle," Lenore began, "who has been with us a year now, and who has given us all such joy and such pride."

Isabelle dimpled. "I love you, Nanna."

"I love you, too, dear. And now a toast to Nathan and Caitlin, who will be adding another precious new member to our family in a few months."

Nathan and Caitlin beamed blissfully while Isabelle bounced in her seat in anticipation of her playmate.

Lenore continued. "To Gideon, whose latest book has just hit the bestseller list. And to Adrienne, who helped him get there."

Everyone politely applauded the accomplishment. Gideon leaned over to give his wife a smacking kiss on the cheek, which, coming from him, was a truly romantic gesture, Deborah thought mistily.

Lenore turned finally to motion toward Deborah and Dylan. "To Deborah and her new business venture with Lindsey. May they find all the success they so richly deserve. And to Dylan, my newest son, who has just sold his first novel."

"Again, thanks to Adrienne," Gideon couldn't resist pointing out.

"Mostly definitely thanks to Adrienne," Dylan acknowledged willingly.

"I'm sure it will be the first of many," Lenore said confidently. And then she raised her glass again. "To family."

Deborah's smile was as bright as anyone's in the room when she lifted her own glass high. "To family," they all said together.

Dylan's eyes were locked happily, heatedly with Deborah's as they sipped their drinks to seal the sentiment.

* * * * *

Coming soon only from

Silhouette®

SPECIAL EDITION™

The McClouds of MISSISSIPPI

by
GINA WILKINS

After their father's betrayal, the McCloud siblings
hid their broken hearts and drifted apart.
Would one matchmaking little girl be enough
to bridge the distance...and lead them to love?

Don't miss

The Family Plan (SE #1525)
March 2003
When Nathan McCloud adopts a four-year-old, will his sexy
law partner see he's up for more than fun and games?

Conflict of Interest (SE #1531)
April 2003
Gideon McCloud wants only peace and quiet, until
unexpected visitors tempt him with the family of his dreams.

and

Faith, Hope and Family (SE #1538)
May 2003
When Deborah McCloud returns home, will she find her
first, true love waiting with welcoming arms?

Available at your favorite retail outlet. Only from Silhouette Books!

Silhouette®

Where love comes alive™

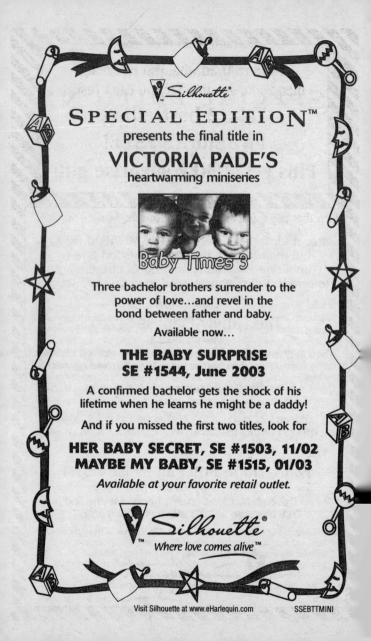

If you enjoyed what you just read,
then we've got an offer you can't resist!

Take 2 bestselling
love stories FREE!
Plus get a FREE surprise gift!

Clip this page and mail it to Silhouette Reader Service™

IN U.S.A.	**IN CANADA**
3010 Walden Ave.	P.O. Box 609
P.O. Box 1867	Fort Erie, Ontario
Buffalo, N.Y. 14240-1867	L2A 5X3

YES! Please send me 2 free Silhouette Special Edition® novels and my free surprise gift. After receiving them, if I don't wish to receive anymore, I can return the shipping statement marked cancel. If I don't cancel, I will receive 6 brand-new novels every month, before they're available in stores! In the U.S.A., bill me at the bargain price of $3.99 plus 25¢ shipping and handling per book and applicable sales tax, if any*. In Canada, bill me at the bargain price of $4.74 plus 25¢ shipping and handling per book and applicable taxes**. That's the complete price and a savings of at least 10% off the cover prices—what a great deal! I understand that accepting the 2 free books and gift places me under no obligation ever to buy any books. I can always return a shipment and cancel at any time. Even if I never buy another book from Silhouette, the 2 free books and gift are mine to keep forever.

235 SDN DNUR
335 SDN DNUS

Name	(PLEASE PRINT)	
Address	Apt.#	
City	State/Prov.	Zip/Postal Code

* Terms and prices subject to change without notice. Sales tax applicable in N.Y.
** Canadian residents will be charged applicable provincial taxes and GST.
   All orders subject to approval. Offer limited to one per household and not valid to
   current Silhouette Special Edition® subscribers.
   ® are registered trademarks of Harlequin Books S.A., used under license.

SPED02   ©1998 Harlequin Enterprises Limited

Silhouette®

SPECIAL EDITION™

Continues the captivating series
from *USA TODAY* bestselling author

SUSAN MALLERY

HOMETOWN HEARTBREAKERS

**These heart-stoppin' hunks are rugged,
ready and able to steal your heart!**

Don't miss the next irresistible books in the series...

COMPLETELY SMITTEN
On sale February 2003
(SE #1520)

ONE IN A MILLION
On sale June 2003
(SE #1543)

Available at your favorite retail outlet.

Silhouette®

Where love comes alive™

COMING NEXT MONTH